The Blood Red Ruby

Voodoo Rumors 1951

The Blood Red Ruby

Voodoo Rumors 1951

By D. Alan Lewis

The Blood Red Ruby

Voodoo Rumors 1951

Published by D. Alan Lewis and
Voodoo Rumors Media

Interior and Cover by D. Alan Lewis

Voodoo Rumors Media
Nashville, Tennessee 37211

Acknowledgements

Special thanks to my beta readers, especially Tad Beaty, Erica Fey, Michelle Franzen, and Kimberly Mayfield.

Special thanks to Adam Shaw for the original artwork, which served as inspiration.

And thanks to my children for giving me a purpose in life, and occasionally, high blood pressure.

Author's Notes

The original version of 'The Blood Red Ruby' and the world of Thomas Dietrich began as a short story for a Halloween writing contest, many years ago. A year later, it was included in the anthology, 'Midnight Movie Creature Feature Vol.2'.

I thought that was the end of the story, but for years afterwards, I kept coming back to Dietrich and his world. Finally I decided to do more with him. This story was expanded from the original and serves as the opening for a series of short novels, revolving around Thomas Dietrich, a Nashville detective who deals with some odd cases.

Nashville is the perfect place for a paranormal series, being filled with history and out-of-the way places where unknown secrets lay.

Many of the places that appear in this and upcoming books are real. Some places existed in the 1950's and others did not. Some names have been changed to protect the guilty as well as the innocent. It wouldn't be hard to drive about the city and find the locations of many settings in the stories.

If you do, let me know.

D. Alan Lewis

ONE

February 1951

She looked at me with big round eyes, so innocent that I couldn't imagine her line of work requiring her clothing to litter the floors of Nashville's brothels. Coming in from the cold, she twirled like a dancer as her jacket and scarf were removed in haste, and folded neatly over her arm. Her gaze flashed briefly around the bar, and I could see her mentally sizing each man up.

Those brown orbs came back my way and locked on to me. Her incisors bit down on her lower lip and I could see a hint of reluctance in her step. Approaching with feigned confidence, she motioned to the worn red-leather seat across the table and looked at me with a pleading expression.

Nodding, I tried not to stare at the girl as she took a seat, but something about her kept my attention. Her dark red dress clung tight to her subtle curves, and then tighter still as she slid into the booth. Blondie was just another working girl, hustling on Nashville's streets and looking for a score, but she was obviously new to Jerry's bar and from her nervous mannerisms, new to the job.

Having spent the past several years living in whatever bottle cost the least, I'd gotten to know the girls – nonprofessionally, of course - who worked the nearby corners and frequented this dive. I wouldn't deny that I'm a man with needs, but paying for bedroom fun wasn't my style.

It seemed obvious that she was trying pull off that youthful teenage appearance that some men like. Being a man who solves puzzles and reads people for a living, I pegged her age somewhere around twenty-five.

Her lips twitched as she nervously asked, "Do you always drink alone?"

Yep, this one was new to the biz. A professional always starts with a compliment to break the ice with a prospective John. Something to make them feel special and, in a sad way, feel wanted.

"Only on certain nights."

"Oh," she whispered. After a moment, as if garnering up courage, Blondie asked a little louder,

"Which nights are special?"

I lifted my glass, mocking a toast, "All of them, lately."

"Hope you don't mind, but I need to get off my feet for a little while and all the stools were taken. Between my dancing gig and this…"

She paused and smiled at me. "Besides, you looked lonely, so I thought you may want some… company."

Her lips were painted cherry-red and the dim lights hanging overhead made them glisten in a seductive way. While most men would prefer those lips doing something other than talking, I felt the need for a nice conversation this evening. It'd been a long day. Hell, it'd been a long year. Some company might bring me out of my self-imposed depression. Of course, she could take off once she realized I wasn't interested in playtime; my need for carnal activities had been buried a while back alongside my late wife.

"Don't mind the gruff manners. I've had a couple of drinks and a run of bad luck as of late." I tilted my head and took another sip. "You have a beautiful voice. Soft and feminine. I'd say you're from someplace east of here. Maybe Knoxville or the Smokey Mountains?

Her mouth dropped open in surprise followed by an expression of disappointment. "Yes, east of here. I'm sorry. I've been trying hard to lose my accent. A music agent told me that I'd have better luck if I sounded more Midwestern."

Despite her efforts, every word she spoke sounded like it'd been soaked in the type of accent that you only hear in the wilds of East Tennessee. I'm not saying that it made her sound like some sort of a country hick. On the contrary, the twang in her words added a country charm that many men, including myself, drool over.

She gave a smile and tilted her head as she studied me. "You have... um, you have nice eyes. But they look so sad, so empty."

"Look around, Pumpkin." I took a long sip of my whiskey. "Everyone in here has that look. Some lost everything back in '29 and never recovered. Some guys are lonely and spend their meager paychecks hiring a girl for a few hours. You know the type. The kind with faces that only a mother could love, who desperately need a woman to show them some attention. *Any* kind of attention. You see Floyd over there, back in the far-left booth?"

She leaned slightly, looking back over her shoulder. It took a moment but she nodded. I noticed her face wrinkle a little in disgust.

"Yea, I'm sure he gets that look a lot. He got burnt up pretty bad in the war. Lots of scars on his face and neck. The son of a bitch won a medal for running back and forth through a burning building over and over to save some injured men, to save his buddies. Had to carry them out one or two at a time. His clothing caught fire on his way out with the last one. Spent months in the hospital recovering, just wanting to get home to his blushing bride. His wife left him as soon as he got back. The hussy told him that she couldn't put up with that kind of ugly."

I paused and took a sip, hoping the alcohol would keep my mind from thinking about my own pain from the war, both the physical kind and the mental.

"How's that for a homecoming? Nowadays, he pays a regular girl to sit with him and just talk. Sad, isn't it? It takes cash just to get a woman to sit and talk with him."

Her eyes lowered and looked at her hands as she mulled over the comment. I wondered if she'd been asked to do something like that - to give a man what he really needs, something other than a romp in the hay. It seemed doubtful that she knew the world could be so damn cold and cruel.

I sighed, realizing my words sounded mean. "Damn it. I'm sorry. I wasn't trying to make you feel guilty or anything. Floyd and I served on different sides of the world during the war, but I feel like we both went through the same hell, in one form or another."

"And why do you have that look? The empty look?"

"Well, some of us just can't bear living from day to day without a little assistance." I raised my glass at the last part, gave it a shake, letting what remained of the ice cubes tinkle against the sides, and then took another sip.

This young woman was as much a hooker as I was. A traveler, lost in the big city with no job, no man, and squat for cash... I'd seen it a hundred times, but she had something different. She had eyes that made men want to talk to her, had looks that made men want to hold her, and her beauty was as innocent as new-fallen snow…

Of course, in this city, even the whitest snow tinges as soon as it hits the grime of the streets.

Those eyes kept drawing me in for some reason I couldn't figure out, and then it finally struck me. The hair, nose, and lips were different, but those eyes sparkled just like my late wife's did. The perfect shade of brown with golden flakes sprinkled about. The longer I looked into them, the stronger a mental voice whispered something that I knew I'd regret.

You can save her.

"New to Nashville?" I asked.

Her blonde curls danced as she quickly nodded.

"I came to town to break into the music biz. I wanna be a backup singer - well, maybe start there and see where I can go. Everyone back home says I've got the pipes to make it to the big time. I've met a couple of men who know folks."

"I bet you have," I interrupted, almost growling in anger.

The words weren't meant to be mean, but I regretted saying them as soon as they left my mouth. Her expression conveyed that I wasn't the first to say something along those lines and that she worried that everyone might be right.

A young woman comes to Nashville, the Music City, meets a few so-called 'nice men' who are willing to help a pretty little girl out. Then reality sets in, and she sees that they only want to make a little music between her thighs. And in the end, she winds up working the streets or working for one of the brothels for enough cash to survive. I'd seen it before and it never gets easier to watch the spiraling descent of a girl's hopes and dreams until she's reduced to a two-bit whore or, worse, a drug-laced corpse.

I gave her a reassuring smile and raised my glass again. "I hope they really are able to get you in with someone in the biz. Here's to your success, babe."

She seemed to avoid looking at me. "I know that I must seem pretty... pathetic. This isn't what I was planning on doing for a living. Just seems that no one out there will give a new girl a chance. I got into town a few weeks ago, ran out of money a few days ago. I have gig at the Black Poodle Lounge, dancing four nights a week."

"The strip joint?"

She spoke meekly. "Yes, I..."

She paused and looked at me. When she spoke again, her voice took on a defiant tone.

"Look, I love performing. Dancing, singing, and yes, even stripping. Some may think it's shameful, but I really like being seen, getting all the attention. When I'm on the stage, I'm in charge. At least in the club, the men aren't touching me."

"I wasn't judging you."

"Sorry. Seems like men are either wanting to screw me for cash or judging every decision I make."

She let out a huff and then sat back and relaxed somewhat. "Money at the club has been tight this week, so I thought I might make a little extra money, assuming I found a man or two I liked. You know, someone handsome, gentle, and who isn't a pervert."

Her eyes studied my glass. The amber liquid looked inviting but tasted like crap. Work had been slow as of late, so my usual Jameson sat just out of my price range. Instead, something cheap numbed my senses and warmed my gut.

I noticed her trembling hands as she tried to make herself look comfortable, trying not to appear to be as young and desperate as she really was. I knew what she wanted and it wasn't to provide the usual service.

I nodded to the barkeep, pointed to the glass, and held up two fingers.

"You got a name, Handsome?" she asked, looking down at her fidgeting fingers. They gently tapped on the table in rhythm to some unheard tune playing in her head. When I didn't answer, her gaze moved back to mine.

"Dietrich. Thomas Spencer Dietrich. My sister calls me Thomas, everyone else just calls me Dietrich. And no one, other than my mother, calls me Tommy." I drained the last of the whisky from my glass.

"Married?" She half-heartedly pointed in the direction of my left hand and the gold band that still cut into my ring finger, the one that had remained there for far too long.

"I was."

"She leave you or you leave her?"

Her big round eyes were so sweet. The working girls usually would ask a few questions, get into a man's mind if he didn't immediately pony up money for a romp or a long wet kiss down below, but this girl didn't seem the type to ask without sincerely wanting to know.

I gave in to the question with a brief whisper. "Neither."

"I don't understand…"

My hand was halfway to the table with the glass when I stopped and narrowed my eyes, letting her know that wasn't something I wanted to explain. Her eyes opened wide as it struck her. The shocked expression turned to one of pity, a look I hated whenever I got it. She tried to smile and gave a nod of understanding.

Like instinct, my thumb rubbed the gold band as I looked into those brown eyes. "You got a name, Doll-Face?"

"Honey." Then she glanced around, as if worried someone was listening in on our conversation. "Well, the other girls, you know - dancers at the club - said I should use a name like that. A name that men would like. You know, something sexy. My real name is Natalie. Natalie Knight."

I gave a nod.

"I'm not sure why I told you that."

I lifted my glass and feigned another toast. "Glad to make your acquaintance, Natalie. Or would you prefer me to call you Honey?"

"Please, Natalie is fine. So… is that what made your life so…" She shifted about, searching for a word that she hoped wouldn't insult or hurt me.

I found it amusing, but decided to help the poor thing out.

"Empty? Hun, losing a wife a few years back is part of it, but just part. Putting my Momma in the ground a couple of months ago didn't help either."

"I'm so sorry," she whispered. "I hope she had a good life."

I blinked, not knowing how to respond to that. Although her heart stopped ticking two months back, she'd mentally died many years ago. Seeing what had happened to her only daughter had broken her heart and snapped something in the old girl's head.

Years earlier, my little sister had fallen in with the wrong crowd, a sect of Devil-worshipping cultists. Then, in a fit of vengeance against me, a demon they'd tried to summon and control spirited her off to the underworld and reshaped her into something horrific. After Lily's transformation and return from Hell, Momma just stopped talking, stopped moving, and spent the rest of her days in an asylum just outside of Nashville.

When I'd go to see her, she didn't even seem to know I was there. Momma would just sit in her rocking chair, humming a tune from my childhood, and staring through the wall at some other world where her family was all together, safe from the insanity of this reality. My weekly visits never felt like enough when she was alive and now that she had left, that guilt of never being able to reach her since she'd mentally collapsed in on herself gnawed at me.

"What did you mean, when you said that their passing was only part of it?" she asked.

Jerry, the bartender and owner of this place, sat our drinks in front of us.

I gave a nod of appreciation. "Thanks, Jer'." The tall scarecrow with slicked-back gray hair nodded and left us. I lifted the glass to my lips and took a quick sip, but even Jerry's finest rotgut couldn't distract me for long from the blonde puppy-dog sitting across the booth.

"There are things I see in my line of work..."

I hesitated before continuing. I really wasn't sure she'd believe me.

"Listen. I've seen crap that would make you question everything you ever learned in school or in church. Stuff that'll make you wonder if the good Lord even exists or if He's sitting on high and laughing at our misery. This place, the very soil this city sits on, is soaked in evil."

I held up the glass again, letting the spirits swirl around inside. "No matter how hard I try, how hard I fight the darkness, the evil never goes away. The papers rarely talk about it, never let on that monsters and vampires and such even exist… well, most of the time, anyway. You ask why I'm drinking alone every night. It's all just a long, crazy story and it's something that'll keep you up at night." I paused and let out a breath I didn't realize I'd been holding.

"Scary?"

She looked at her glass apprehensively, but I wasn't sure if it was the alcohol or my words that had her spooked. Then those beautiful brown eyes turned and looked me over, studying what type of man I was.

She bit her lip. "Can I hear it? Your story, I mean. I… I really don't want to go back out tonight. And, I'd like to hear more about you. What made you the man you are?"

She reached over and cupped her hand over my empty one. Her flesh felt electrifying. It'd been a while since I lost her, lost my wife. Thoughts of her touching me, placing her hand over mine all those years ago when I proposed marriage, rushed to the forefront of my thoughts. I shifted in my seat and tried not to let the emotions show. Absent-mindedly, my thumb kept twisting the gold band on my ring finger, the way it always did when I felt guilty about looking at other women.

"Please," she whispered. "You seem like the only

good man I've met in a long while."

Her words were meant as a compliment… at least, I hoped they were.

I scoffed, relieved that her foolish misconceptions of me could push away the memories. Of course, those thoughts were replaced by others from the decadent teenage years, the ones I had spent as a would-be criminal.

"Good man? Hun, I've never been a good man. Though maybe I'm better then I used to be… I started off on the bad side of the tracks, but certain things out there can scare the worst of us straight."

I looked into those eyes again. The innocence of her short life seemed to well up in them. Clearly, she had no idea of the horrors that infest this city, like so many other dark spots around the world. She knew nothing of the harbingers of evil that stalked the streets, filled the shadows, and corrupted or consumed the flesh of little girls like her.

She needed to know. She should know what lurks in the Music City after dark, if she was going to survive here.

I sat my glass on the table and thought about the best way to tell the story. "I'll tell you, but you need to understand that what I tell you is the truth, every word."

Again, she nodded.

"It all may have happened a couple of decades ago, but I feel like that night has stayed with me, aged me, turned me old before my time. I've never seen the world the same since. And I guess it's fitting to tell you this story, since you want to know how my life really started."

TWO

The Ford V8 roadster slid to a stop in front of the solitary bank in this godforsaken little town. Four of us poured out of it fast, like the thing was on fire. Benny, our tried and true driver, stayed behind the wheel with a pistol in hand. The man could drive faster and better than anyone alive, and he loved his Colt .45 automatic almost as much as he treasured his Ford.

"If the bastards show their ugly pig faces around here, I'm gonna open up on 'em," Benny said. He popped open his door a tad and placed one foot on the ground, readying himself for a gun battle.

"Don't go and draw any unwarranted attention, you shit!" I yelled over my shoulder at him.

If the coppers arrived at one of our robberies before we'd left the building, he'd fire some shots, forcing them to keep their distance. Any gunfire would alert those of us inside the place that time was up. We knew better then to actually kill a cop, but Benny had grown bolder with each robbery. We worried that it was only a matter of time, and Lord knows we didn't need the sort of attention that would bring.

"Like we practiced, boys. This one isn't any different from the others. Just stick to the plan," John, our fearless leader, hurriedly shouted as we, that is Jimmy, Mikey, and I took the steps leading up into the bank two at a time.

We had a good routine, one that we'd practiced a lot. All the details of each job had to be considered and alternatives weighed and planned for before we made the attempt. I'd spent a few months in jail, a year earlier. I may have only been sixteen at the time, but an ill-tempered God-fearing judge tossed me in the state pen with the adults. The old timers loved to talk about their exploits to pass the time and would teach little snots like me the fine art of robbing banks. Eager punks such as myself listened close and learned how to watch the goings-on, time out the movements and routines of the guards, figure out the best times to hit 'em, and, most importantly, find the fastest way to get across the state or county line. The boys in blue can't keep chasing you if you've crossed out of their jurisdiction. And without decent radios, no one else in the neighboring counties or states would know to be on the lookout.

While some gangs would hit three or four banks a day, we took our time and plotted every move. It'd worked every time so far and we didn't see any reason why things would be different today. Rushed jobs usually meant small hauls, but we'd always come out with several grand.

We'd already hit a bank in Memphis two days before and were gone before the cops even knew about it, just like we'd planned. Today's job was to take whatever cash we could from this little waste-of-space village, located right outside the Memphis city limits, and then we'd hightail it home to Nashville to spend it on bad moonshine and two-dollar whores.

Our gang always walked, never ran, into a bank. Running tells everyone you're scared and want the job over quick. Walking will let them know you've done this before, and that you're a professional. When people see you're scared or in a hurry, they get defiant and tend to do stupid things, like trying to be a hero. Being stupid like that gets people killed. Acting like a professional keeps folks calm and thinking clearly about the what-ifs that can come from being too brave. What-ifs like getting their chest pumped full of hot lead.

Of Course, professionals don't kill unless they have to… well, except Benny.

"Hands up, people!" John shouted, making sure his Tommy gun was visible to all. "We're only here for the bank's money, not yours. So stay calm, keep quiet, and let us do our jobs and everyone'll live in the end."

Jimmy and Mikey strolled from teller to teller, having each one fill up our white canvas bags with all the cash from their drawers. John stayed back at the front door, holding his gun and watching the whole scene, ready to pop off a shot or two or thirty if necessary. And me, I kept my machine gun pointed at the fat guard who I'd backed into a corner. The round old man had more sweat seeping out of him than the Mississippi after a hard April rain.

"Keep those hands up where I can see 'em." I spoke calmly and didn't make any aggressive moves. My attitude drew fear from the guard, but he could also see that I wouldn't be a danger unless he provoked me.

There were a couple of old folks - customers, I reckon - who had the bad luck of being there at the wrong time. But we had a routine and we stuck to it, at least for the moment. See, we never stole anything from the people, only the bank. It's a good way of keeping the public on our side. Most folks figured that the bankers lost their money or took it away when the stock market crashed in '29. So, as we saw it, those fat-cat bankers deserved to shell out the greenbacks to the needy folks like us. We never took anything from the needy or from anyone who happened to be in the banks while we were robbing them, for that matter. That just didn't seem like it'd be fair. Like Robin Hood, we only stole from the rich, and we gave to the poor... though, of course, with our spending habits when it came to booze and dames, our pockets were never overflowing for long.

But this day, our routine fell apart. An old lady - I'd later find out her name was Betty - stood in one of the lines, looking at the lot of us through a defiant expression and matching stance. The woman wore a lovely flower-print dress and a big ruby necklace that caught the light, sending sparkles that everyone in the bank must've seen. The rock must've been the size of a half-dollar, and it was all wrapped up in braided gold wire.

I can honestly say that it was the prettiest damn thing I'd ever seen. Thing was, it was also the prettiest damn thing that John had ever seen, because he walked right up to her and yanked it off her neck. As little and frail as the old bird appeared, I'm surprised that her head didn't pop off from the hard tug it took to get the chain's clasp to snap.

"John! Careful!" I couldn't help but blurt out the warning. I was worried that he might've hurt the old girl.

"You give that back, you filthy thing!" Betty had one of those high squeaky voices that you only hear on radio shows or cartoons in the theaters. "You ain't got no right to take that!"

John laughed at her tenacity while the boys finished up with the tellers. They yelled back and forth, making sure every cash drawer had been emptied and bagged. Once certain that we'd gotten all we could, Jimmy, Mikey, and I started backing up toward the front door to make ourselves ready to go. My gun stayed trained on the guard, and he had the smarts not to make any moves.

The old girl kept hollering, "My late husband of fifty years gave that to me! He'll be making sure you'll return it! He'll burn ya if you try to keep it! You aren't the first to try and steal it! It always comes back to me!"

I caught a brief look at her expression as I started out the door, an expression of sheer unadulterated hatred. A chill ran down my spine. *We're lucky her husband isn't around anymore,* I thought. After all, she did say 'late husband'.

Once outside, I dove in the back of the Ford with Jimmy and Mikey close behind, John leapt into his usual place, up front next to Benny.

"Go, go, go!" we shouted.

Benny hesitated. I knew what he wanted—a cop to show up so he could get a shot or two before tearing out of town.

John reached over and slapped him hard across the back of the head. "Go, shithead!" he shouted.

Benny slammed the gearshift forward, floored the gas pedal, and the V8 screamed as it lurched forward, throwing us all back in our seats. The words that Betty shouted as we left kept ringing in my ears as we sped out of town.

The siren of a cop car, still a long way off, sounded off, but the Ford's engine roared like an angry lion and left a thick cloud of dust in our wake. We knew they'd never catch up, but I didn't like the amount of dust stirred up by the tires. Seemed to me that we were leaving a visible trail, hanging strangely in the air for longer than it should've, perfect for the cops to follow.

I decided it couldn't be helped. Benny did drive like a madman, after all, keeping that pedal down on the floorboard and making the wheels spin faster than a souped-up tornado.

John sat back and relaxed, laughing. "Did you see that bitch's eyes when we left? Well, that little old thing didn't need a big-ass rock like this weighing her down, anyhow. I'm surprised it didn't break her back, lugging this thing around."

He held that ruby up and looked at it, letting it spin so that it filled the car with glimmering red light.

"This thing has writing on it. Well, not writing, just strange symbols etched on to each facet. Can't make out what any of them are." He stared deeply into the jewel.

I watched for a while as the swaying of the car made the jewel move back and forth. That, plus the way the thing sparkled and I swear the thing had John hypnotized. For a moment. I could've sworn his jaw even went slack for a moment.

Jimmy kept looking back at that cop all nervous and jumpy-like, barking out reports of the distance between us. Mikey was pulling the cash from the bags, trying to count it all out. I was wedged between the two.

Stealing a glance at my hands, I realized I was shaking. Normally, robbing a bank didn't affect me at all, and especially not like this. Something just didn't feel right to me about the whole thing. I'm usually not the nervous type, never have been, but the cops didn't usually stay on our tail that long and John's expression was spooking me. He was enthralled by that damn rock, like it'd put a spell on him.

"Don't do that here," I said to Mikey as he started piling up the bills by denomination on his lap. "Wait till we're well and clear of Memphis and we shake these cops lose. You know they'll be calling every county in the western half of the state, telling them to be on the lookout for us."

Benny laughed. "Takes too much time to make those calls."

Mikey ignored me, so I glanced back at the red stone still dangling from John's outstretched hand. An eerie coldness came over me and it felt like the whole world just turned to ice. For the briefest moment, I swore I saw my breath, like a mist emanating from my nostrils on the coldest day in winter.

All of a sudden, all four wheels on the Ford just locked in place and stopped turning. We were thrown forward as the car slid. The sounds of metal creaking, the tires scraping on the loose dirt and rock, and the sudden roaring surge of the engine deafened me momentarily as we came to an unexpected stop. John smacked the windshield so hard that it shattered. I swear I heard the cracking of Benny's ribs on the steering wheel as the force of the deceleration pushed him into it. As for me and the boys in the back, we got tossed about and shaken up, but were no worse for wear. For a moment, pictures of dead presidents printed in green, black, and white hovered in mid-air before dropping to cover everything.

Benny popped his door open and rolled out on to the dirt road, groaning the entire way down and holding his right arm close to his ribs. He spoke in broken words, gasping for breath between each one. "What... the hell... happened?"

After reaching over and shoving the passenger door open, I climbed over Jimmy and jumped out the passenger side of the car. Pulling the front door open, I saw blood pouring out of John's forehead. He'd been wedged in a fetal position between the front seat and the dashboard. Grabbing his shoulders, I pulled until he could push himself out. He staggered out of the car, holding a blood-covered hand to his forehead.

I grabbed a handkerchief from my back pocket, pulled his hand back, and pushed the weathered cloth against the gash over his right eye, trying to stop the flow of blood. He tried to fight for a second, but when he saw the bright red blood soaked into what had been a white cloth, all resistance left him. I made him stand still while I tried to get the bleeding to stop or at least slow down.

I shot a glare at Benny. "Benny, what the hell? We've got coppers back yonder."

Benny groaned and huffed as he got back in and turned the key several times, but all we heard were clicks from under the hood. He cursed a good bit with each attempt, finally yelling out, "It's dead! Don't know why, but she's dead."

"Mikey!" I shouted. "Grab up that cash a little faster, will ya, the cops are coming. We gotta head up the hill over there and lose ourselves in the woods."

John took the hanky from me, pushed it harder against his wound, and looked around. Shaking his head, he seemed to finally realize what had happened and the dire straits we found ourselves in.

When he spoke, he barked. "Ain't a house around and the woods are thick. Yeah, good idea. We gotta go, boys."

The car's hood creaked as Benny raised it and looked over the engine. That boy loved his car and wasn't about to give it up and leave it behind. And my hand to God that this is the way it happened -

Without anyone in the contraption, the engine fired up and the car lurched forward with Benny still bent over the grill looking at the thing. The engine's sudden roar scared all of us and we jumped back, not realizing that Benny hadn't started it at first. He couldn't move fast enough and the Ford's movement knocked him down on his back. He jerked, trying to roll away when the driver's side tire mounted his chest. And just as suddenly as it had happened, the car's engine just shut off, leaving the tire perched on top of him.

Now, you know that a V8 Ford isn't a light thing and a man's ribs can only do so much. The crunching of bone and flesh made me feel sick. Benny didn't scream, just made this loud burping sound as all the air was immediately squeezed out of him at once, blasting out in a booming of air and blood. The boy couldn't even talk, couldn't get any air into his flattened lungs. He just laid there as we ran to him, slowly moving his arms and trying to push the damned thing off of himself. His lips opened and closed, like a fish out of the water, desperately needing breath.

The pressure on his chest made his eyes bulge out and they moved back and forth, looking at all of us before he stopped moving. I knew he was dead, but those eyes didn't close. He just stared up with a panicked look on his face. That image would fill my nightmares for years to come, the way his expression showed the terror, the fear, and the inability to understand what was happening.

John and Jimmy kept trying to roll it off of him, as if that'd have mattered at that point, but those wheels were locked solid again. Benny's pride and joy wouldn't move an inch.

We remembered our other troubles real fast when the police siren got louder. Grabbing our stuff, we ran as fast as we could across the road. I turned around when I heard tires sliding to a stop in the dirt. The two policemen jumped out of their black-and-white and shot like mad in our direction. They didn't mean to catch us, so much as gun us down and display our bodies for the newsreel cameras.

I didn't want to stay for a fight, so I kept running for higher ground. I figured that we could lose ourselves in the trees and pick them off one at a time, if they were dumb enough to chase after us. John was smart enough to do the same. Mikey ran like a bat out of hell. He had a money bag tucked under his arm and was protecting it like a running back carrying a football. He worried so much about losing the money that he'd forgotten to grab his gun.

Now, Jimmy, on the other hand, was never one to do the smart thing. He had a BAR—a Browning Automatic Rifle - and he was letting that baby roar. The thing is an oversized rifle with a twenty-round clip that can fire full auto, spraying big chunks of lead through the best body-armor the cops have. Boom, boom, boom… if you've never heard one of them being shot, then you don't understand the effect that has on people.

Looking back over my shoulder, I saw him blast

one of the cops in the chest a couple of times, killing him almost instantly. One shot from a .30-06 will take down a bull, but he wasn't taking any chances. I think he may have winged the other one in the arm, but shooting a BAR on the run means no chance for accuracy.

Turning and shouting something obscene, he let the BAR roar for a bit, smiling the whole time. He yelped when a lone bullet from a police revolver hit him in his gut.

Grunting and wrapping an arm around the .38 caliber slug in his stomach, he staggered up the hill and followed behind John as more cop cars slid to a stop beside the broken-down Ford.

I knew the surviving cop knew where we went into the wood. They knew we were wounded and had limited guns and ammo, to say nothing of no way of getting out of the county. How would we get out of this alive?

THREE

Well, it was around lunchtime when the car died and we took to the woods. We were on foot and didn't stop moving until the sun was partially obscured by the horizon. Six hours of constant trudging up and down hilly terrain can wear out any man. By late afternoon, the idea of riding in a car - even a police car - had me secretly hoping we'd get caught. I just didn't want to move anymore. My feet and legs felt numb from exhaustion and every part of me had scrapes and scratches from all the tree limbs and bushes that seemed to be razor-sharp.

The gash on John's head wouldn't stop bleeding. I guess all the moving and such kept his blood pumping too hard for the wound to clot up. It wasn't gushing or anything, but just kept leaking, running down into his eyes.

He seemed to be constantly cursing and wiping, repeating the actions a few minutes later. His face and shirt were stained red. To this day, I wonder how he didn't just bleed to death out there in the wood.

"You gonna keep up with us, Jimmy?" I shouted back to our wounded straggler.

"Dadgum cops!" he hollered between pants. "Can't keep running this hard with a bullet in my gut. Hurts like hell. Each step I take feels like a hornet keeps stinging my insides."

"Think he'll make it?" I asked John in a whispered voice. I knew Jimmy was far enough back and couldn't hear my concerns. Last thing we needed was for him to go all crazy and such about the Grim Reaper coming for him. He'd always been paranoid about spiritual stuff.

"Tied that shirt of his around him a while back. Learned 'bout making field dressings when I was in the Great War, ya know. That stopped the bleedin', but if we can't find a doc to pull that slug out of 'im … I don't know. I saw men in Germany last for days with a gut wound. Others only make it for minutes. No way of knowing."

We looked at one another and both nodded, knowing that another friend was going to be lost soon unless a miracle happened.

Looking over his shoulder, John shouted over to Mikey, "Still got my money, boy?"

Mikey only grunted and kept his head down. He'd been quiet ever since Benny's demise. The two of them had always acted more like brothers then friends.

Wiping the sweat from my brow, I looked over to John. "Great War. I was born the month it started."

I laughed, but I only got a dirty look from the old man. John had a couple more decades on his age than I did, but you'd not know it at first glance. He attributed his youthful look to clean living, but given the amount of booze he drank, I found that laughable.

Glancing up, I could just make out the darkening blue sky. Its weak light didn't make it to the base of the trees, so the ground lost all texture and just became this black unknown thing that we charged across.

"Can't see a bloomin' thing with no sunlight," John said, looking around. "This is as good a place as any to stop for the night. Already starting to get a chill in the air."

So we stopped and built a little fire. My stomach was so empty that I figured the cops in the next county could hear it rumbling.

"We need food and water, in a bad way," Mikey said in a way that we all knew always annoyed John.

"There're plenty of squirrels about," I suggested.

John stomped his foot down.

"Are you out of your damn mind? What are you gonna do, plug some tree rodents with your pistol? Maybe just open up on one with a Tommy and do a little sprayin' and prayin'?" He jabbed his finger in my chest. "That kinda shit is why you'll never have your own gang. You're not thinking straight. One shot, let alone several, will lead the cops right to us."

Thinking back, I don't know if it would've mattered. We were all so hungry that we wanted to take the chance. But he said no and we all did as we were told.

We kept the fire small so that its light and smoke wouldn't travel far in the heavy woods. John held the ruby necklace up and let the jewel spin around.

"Bet this thing is worth a pretty penny."

The cuts on the stone, glistening in the firelight, made little patterns of red and black dance back and forth across his face. I thought about how pretty that would be on a girl like my sweetie Laurissa, but on John's weathered face, it made him look like the Devil himself.

I had to speak up. "John? I don't think you should have taken it."

He looked at me, the firelight still casting an eerie glow onto his face. His eyes seemed to sparkle the same way the ruby did.

"That's why I'm in charge of you and you're the bottom man in the group. You don't have enough sense to know what's worth the effort. A rock like this is worth a bag full of cash, and a hell of a lot easier to carry."

He turned away and held the rock up again to stare into it. "I'll find someone to sell it to, maybe a fence in Nashville." He emitted a hushed dark laugh that put my nerves on edge. "Maybe I'll use it to pay one of those high-class hookers. A woman of beauty and elegance. The type of girl that the fat cats keep on the side in those pretty little bungalows, far away from their wives."

His voice lowered to a whisper. "They can't say no when I shove this down their throats. They'll have to take me seriously."

Mikey, who'd spent seemingly every minute counting the cash, looked up so fast he could've gotten whiplash. "You better damn well fence it and split all that cash with the rest of us. We're a team, remember?"

John slowly turned to face him and I saw anger flash in his eyes. "What?"

Mikey reared up in a way that I'd never seen him do. "I said, you sell it and split the money with us. That's the way things work in a gang. We split the bank's cash, we split the ruby money."

John pulled his pistol from the back of his pants and placed it on his knee. He stared at Mikey as if daring him. "I've not said I would sell it, yet. And if I do, the money is mine. I'm the one who had the sense of mind to snap it off that bitch's neck."

He continued talking about his plans for the ruby, but I couldn't think anymore. My body felt too tired to concentrate on anything other than laying down and praying for sleep or death. Took me a damn long time to finally fall asleep, laying on the cold dirt and leaves. Something about John really bothered me. No… it scared me.

When my eyes finally closed, I didn't get a peaceful rest. I must've rolled back and forth the whole time I was down. Ever since I was a kid, I always worried that bugs would crawl in my ears or up my nose if I slept outside. Every little twig or rock that I felt underneath me would make me jump.

Still, I must have been out for a while… that is, until someone shook me awake and muttered, "Get your ass up."

Mikey's voice was low, almost a whisper, but came out with such force that I knew something was terribly wrong. Suddenly, the barks and howls of dogs echoed through the distant trees. A cold chill seized my heart. He didn't have to say anything else.

Jimmy moaned so loud that I bet the dogs wouldn't even need a scent to find us. "I can't... it hurts!"

John cursed and hauled the wounded man to his feet. "You get up or you stay for those dogs to find you. I don't give a damn which, but stop the damned moaning and groaning. You'll end up getting us all killed."

Furious at his dilemma, Jimmy pushed John back, almost knocking him to the ground. I stepped between them as John reared up, looking like he might punch the crap out of the wounded man.

"We don't have time for this," I said, seeing John's expression change. I think he understood that Jimmy acted out of frustration and not malice. A hurt dog is the most dangerous kind. John gave him a nod and we took off.

We tried to run in the darkness but had little success. Only little slivers of light from the moon peeked through the thick canopy of trees and found their way to the leaf-covered ground. It was enough to help, but not sufficient enough to let us move fast. I think I must've been falling forward or stumbling most of the time we spent rushing.

Jimmy took a nasty spill and rolled down a steep slope until he grabbed a rock to stop himself. The crinkling leaves deafened us and I knew that the sound would give the dogs a better idea of where we were.

"My gun, I can't find my gun," Jimmy said in a hushed but panicked manner. The machine gun had disappeared, lost somewhere in the blackness of the leaf-covered slope.

"I got mine. Just get your ass up and move. That posse will be on us any time now," John said as he tried to lead us in the best direction to keep the dogs at our backs.

The ground was becoming steeper and harder to climb. Then we got into real trouble.

A man's voice shouted from behind, far enough back that it came to me like a whisper. "Let 'em go, boys! They got a good scent. They ain't far off."

"Shit!" John groaned. We sped up only to run smack-dab into an almost vertical slope, with no way around it.

John looked up, mustering up sheer grit. "Gotta go up. Steep enough that the dogs can't climb it. Just look for footholds or anything to grab on to."

I was already halfway up the twenty feet or so, grabbing onto little trees that jutted out of the slope and whatever roots the rains had washed free from the dirt. Mikey threw the money-bag to the top of the slope and scaled the thing like he was part billy-goat.

Surprisingly for a man in his forties, John didn't

break a sweat keeping up with me. At one point, I looked down at him and saw the moisture on his forehead, glistening in the moonlight, on a second glance, I realized that it was more blood from the cut, not perspiration.

Reaching the top, I dropped flat along the edge and held my hand down for John. His fingers felt chilled to the bone when I grabbed his hand and pulled him up to safety. That left Jimmy as the only one still working to get up the embankment.

I could see him clawing at the dirt and trees, pulling himself up, little by little. With each move, he groaned and stopped to clutch his chest and gut tighter. The pain from his wounds must be growing more intense the harder he worked. Each move he made appeared to be a tad slower than the one before. The man was slowly bleeding out. He couldn't have much left in him.

"Don't you bastards leave me!" he shouted. He kept looking back over his shoulders. The sounds of the dogs had closed in on us. We could hear far more than just barks - we could hear the leaves crunching under all those paws as they jumped and ran towards us, zig-zagging through the trees with ease.

First one, then two, and finally ten dogs ran up. They stopped ten feet or so from Jimmy and the embankment, barking and yelping.

The canine cacophony echoed up the slope, sounding loud and painful. The mutts kept calling into the darkness, letting their masters know that they had cornered their prey.

I stretched my hand down as far as I could stretch, trying to reach him, but the act was all in vain. The distance between us was just too great and the harder he tried to pull up and away from the animals, the more he slipped further down.

We couldn't hear the posse stumbling through the dark woods, so we knew there was still hope that he might have enough time to make it up the slope. I figured they were far enough away that they wouldn't be here for another hot minute. Having an idea, I grabbed for my Tommy gun. I'd dropped it when I'd reached the top of the slope. Pulling it snug against my shoulder, I took aim at the dogs and pulled the trigger, but nothing happened.

I tugged at the bolt, but nothing moved. Somehow, the damn thing had jammed. Holding the useless weapon by the stock, I reached down with it and yelled for him to grab the end of the barrel. Jumping a bit, he managed to wrap his fingers around the blued steel, but he yanked so hard that my weapon slipped out my hands and tumbled to the ground below him.

Jimmy, still several feet above the bottom of the

embankment, held onto a root and wrapped the other arm around his wounded gut.

I remember the way he looked up at me, all that pain and fear in his expression. Then something in his face changed. I think he knew what was going to happen. Those eyes of his went wide and he started to cry out. The ground under his feet gave and he slid to the bottom, screaming all the way.

The dogs jumped at him. Their teeth snapped as they advanced, but they never got close enough to attack. Hunting dogs like these were trained to corner and play with the prey, but not kill it. He was trapped and the mutts knew it. Some of the snarling beasts were small beagles and some were large, like retrievers. Jimmy kept his back to the dirt wall and looked around in panic. Picking up my machine gun, he brought it to bear on one of the animals.

One black retriever jumped, clamping its jaws onto Jimmy's arm. Jerking the gun up as he struggled to escape, I saw the barrel pointed in my direction. Without a thought, I jerked my head back away from the edge as he squeezed the trigger. Three shots rang out, throwing hot lead into the tree tops. I jumped, surprised that the weapon fired, considering that it hadn't worked for me moments earlier.

One aspect of a Tommy gun is the bright display of fire that each shot produces. Albeit brief, the brilliant flames as well as the sounds would easily pinpoint our position to the cops. Worse for Jimmy, the weapon's recoil launched it from his weakened hand. The smoking gun fell only a few feet away.

The dogs jumped back from the gunfire, but with the gun on the ground, they inched forward again, growling and stepping to block him from reaching the Tommy again.

Another dog, a big gray bastard, moved closer, baring his teeth and snarling like a creature from Hell. The other dogs seemed to take note of something dark and sinister about him. They stopped their barking and watched it with an apparent uneasiness. They whimpered and stepped away, giving him some room. The beast lowered his head and growled like no dog I've ever heard before.

When I was a kid at church, the God-fearing preacher talked about demons walking the Earth, their appetites and the horrible roars they make. I swear I heard the roar of a demon that evening, demanding flesh and blood to quench its appetites.

Jimmy jumped and started clawing at the slope like a mad man. We knew that dog meant to kill him. Don't ask me how, but we all could sense it. Our wounded friend managed to find some footing and climbed up a few feet up. Mikey and I yelled, pleading for him to move faster.

John screamed, "Don't look back! Just climb up, damn it! Get up here and grab our hands!"

I looked over at John and saw the tears, glistening in the moonlight, rolling down his cheeks. We both leaned as far as we could, stretching out for him, knowing that our friend was doomed.

What I saw next has stayed with me and I think it always will.

The dog jerked, rearing up on its hind legs, standing upright like a person. Bones within its back legs and hindquarters creaked and crackled as they moved out of their customary sockets, adjusting to the new posture. Its head jerked, appearing to momentarily suffer a tremendous amount of pain, but it only lasted for a few seconds. Then the dog glared at Jimmy with an almost human expression. Animals aren't supposed to have those kinds of emotions, but this one just looked at our friend and seemed to revel in Jimmy's predicament and helplessness. Maybe it sounds crazy, but I felt like the beast was happy that the wounded man struggled… it'd make the kill that must more satisfying.

I screamed to Jimmy to climb harder and not look back, but he turned and saw this dog-thing walking towards him. He tore at the dirt till his fingers bled. The dog-thing took a couple of slow careful steps, as if it was testing its balance, and then ran at Jimmy in a blur of movement. Its head twisted to the side and locked around Jimmy's leg. Razor-sharp teeth tore into the meat of his right calf, spraying the ground with his blood. He screamed and his pain echoed through the trees for miles. The dog thrashed its head around and dug its teeth in deeper.

The sickening sounds of teeth scraping against bone tore at my nerves like nails on a blackboard. Blood kept shooting out and I think it induced a kind of bloodlust in the other dogs.

The dog-thing continued thrashing back and forth, sending more torrents of blood and strips of flesh in all directions. With a sharp twist of its head and a loud snap, Jimmy's right leg broke and a few seconds later, the dog-thing wrestled it free from Jimmy completely. My friend screamed and the beast just tossed his prize to the side, slinging blood in all directions.

John raised his machine gun and pulled the trigger. I braced myself for the loud chugging noise, but it just clicked. He started tugging at the bolt, trying to clear the misfired round, but the bolt wouldn't budge. It was as if it'd been welded closed. Frantically, John tried again and again, slowing down as the animals' growls grew louder than Jimmy's screaming. We watched in muted horror as the events unfolded.

Jimmy screamed and rolled back and forth on the blood-soaked ground, and I eventually just couldn't watch anymore. I had to turn away and vomit, but since I had nothing in my stomach, all I managed were a painful series of dry-heaves. The screaming only lasted a few minutes, but felt like an eternity. I thought the dog had killed him.

"Oh God…" Mikey whispered.

His hands moved to cover much of his terror-stricken face and he spoke again in broken words.

"He's—still moving. It—it tore out his—fucking throat."

I looked back down at the carnage. The dog-thing had ripped Jimmy's neck wide open, ensuring he couldn't scream, but it had left him alive to suffer a little longer. It stood over him, watching.

Then the other dogs, seemingly at the dog-thing's unspoken command, launched forward. Their jaws locked onto Jimmy's arms and kept him from resisting as he was slowly ripped open. The dog-thing dug into him like it was digging into loose soil, throwing shredded organs and intestines out into the woods.

I lost my stomach again, spewing bile out onto the ground beside me. I wiped my eyes and made myself look down at my friend, looked beyond the blood and into his glassy eyes. He lay there, helpless and dying, if not already dead. I prayed silently that he'd already left us. I hoped he'd died quickly and drifted far from this place.

When it was all over with, John looked out into the woods behind the bloodbath. He grabbed my arm. "We gotta go."

Mikey just clutched the money-bag and rocked in place. The tone and distance of his voice conveyed his diminished sanity. "Shit ain't right … dang shit ain't right … dogs can't do that … can't walk like people…"

John grabbed Mikey's arm and slapped him hard. "Gotta go now. Those dogs can't climb this hill, but the damn cops can. We've gotta run now."

He was right, of course. Cowards would've run and left their friend behind to be ripped to shreds, but cowards would also be far from here by now. I cursed my compassion for making me stay and try to help instead of thinking of my own skin. I cursed my inability to do something, anything, to help Jimmy and keep my friend alive.

My grand momma always said you reap what you sow, and I'd spent most of my teen years stealing, robbing, and being a despicable excuse for a man. I wondered if this was payback.

FOUR

As we started back up the hillside, I heard the posse moving up the bottom of the slope. They were yelling and spreading out to make sure the cornered man couldn't get away. A couple of minutes later, I heard the first bloodcurdling screams as they found the bloody pieces of him strewn about.

I heard gunshots, a lot of them, as we made our way to the top of the hill. I looked back. I could tell the shots weren't directed at us.

John looked at me and saw my confused expression. "Puttin' down that mad dog," he said. "No, putting down all them dogs, from the sound of it. Ain't gonna worry 'bout that one catching us again."

I couldn't keep the fear from my voice. "What the

hell was that? It wasn't like any dog I've ever seen. I've never seen a dog or any animal do anything like that."

He didn't reply. He didn't know and neither did I. Benny had been run over by his own car and Jimmy killed by that demonic dog-thing. The words of the old woman came back to me.

He'll be making sure you'll return it or he'll burn ya if you try to keep it!

I wondered if Benny and Jimmy were burning in Hell. I wondered if Lucifer had met them at the gates instead of Saint Peter and directed them down to his ring-centric underworld. I wondered if the old woman's husband had carried them there himself.

We walked for hours in the dark, occasionally stumbling and falling. None of us cared about getting hurt. We only wanted to get as far away from the men, the dogs, and Jimmy's blood as we could. Like always, John seemed to know which direction to move. Every time the trees overhead opened enough to let us see the sky, we'd stop and rest while he studied the stars.

I didn't care where we were going, just as long as we kept moving. Ignoring the burning pain of fatigue in my legs, I stayed the course and didn't lag behind, but the occasional stops felt like a godsend.

The ground eventually leveled out, and the trees

opened up onto a stretch of uncultivated flat land. The moonlight gave us a good view of the bluish landscape. About a quarter of a mile away, we could see a farmhouse and, beyond that, a road lined with telephone poles.

Civilization was within reach. Leaving the tree-line behind, we started forward.

In a strange way, it felt like stepping foot into an alien world. The brush-covered stretch was almost as hard to walk across as the dark hills had been. The farm-land hadn't been worked in quite some time and the acres were now covered with whatever weeds could take hold. The house looked smaller then we'd first imagined as we got closer. The little dwelling may have only had a couple of rooms at the most. An outhouse jutted out of the ground on one side. We were downwind of the shithole and the smell from it let us know that it'd been used lately. Someone lived in this dinky little place. I silently prayed they didn't have a phone or a gun.

I waved to John, motioning for us to head toward the street. Staying quiet, he pointed to the house and then pointed to his mouth. I couldn't argue that I needed food as well, but still, I didn't want to take chances. We'd lost two and the old woman's curse felt like it was still running its course.

A beat-up truck sat out in front of the house.

Stepping closer, I whispered to John and Mikey. "Let's just take it and get on the road. We can stop for food after we get across the county line."

He'd been tugging at the bolt on his Tommy gun ever since we left the slope. It hadn't popped open, making the gun useless, but he wouldn't leave it behind. He shot me a look of annoyance.

"Not this late," he said. "Only people that'll be on the roads at this hour are the cops looking for us. They see or hear us and we'll never be able to get away. An old truck like that would never outrun a cop car. No. We'll stay in the house and catch some shuteye till dawn. Maybe the folks will have some food."

I knew he was right. He had a good head about these things. His time in the war had taught him how to survive behind enemy lines. Besides, with our luck, the old rust-bucket might explode if we started it.

Some moaning and panting could be heard as we approached the backdoor. The windows were all wide open, and a woman's moaning made me smile for the first time in a long while. Someone was getting some good lovin' inside and too busy to hear us stomping through the dried brush. The rickety screen door wasn't latched. The hinges squeaked a little as John slowly pulled it open, we grimaced at the noise, but the sounds of lovemaking continued unabated.

The knob turned in his hand, but the wood door didn't budge. Then he smacked his shoulder against it and the door popped right open.

We ran inside and were greeted by the smell of mold and fried chicken. The room appeared bleak and bare in the darkness. A small table sat in a corner with a couple of milk pails turned upside down. I reckoned chairs were in short supply around here. A short countertop was covered with dishes, two of which held the bare chicken bones and scraps of potatoes and carrots. Mikey and I grabbed them up, shoving the uneaten remains of someone's dinner into our empty mouths.

There was a small walled off area that must have been the bedroom. John moved fast to that door and caught the man-of-the-house emerging with a shotgun. One look at John's Tommy gun pointed at him made the naked man lower the weapon and hand it over. It didn't matter if the gun was permanently jammed, no one except us knew it was useless. Looking down the business end of a machine gun was enough to make the bravest of men back down. I couldn't fault the young man for giving up without a fight.

A match behind me fired up and I turned to see Mikey lighting a hurricane lantern. Its warm yellow glow flooded the room, giving me a glimpse of the house. A few wood crates sitting about and a dirty white sheet hanging over the window made up the living room's décor. It became clear really quick that they didn't own the place. Considering how many people did it, I figured they were just squatters, staying here until the law ran them off.

"Come on out here," John said and jerked the man through the doorway. "You too, sweetie, but put something on first."

I couldn't see much, but the lantern's light gave me a glimpse of the woman's nude backside before the dress dropped over her head and covered it up. John just stood in the door, watching. I envied him, the sight must have been a nice distraction from the horrors we'd seen earlier.

"What are we gonna do?" Mikey asked, as he leaned against a wall and stared out the window. "That thing is gonna follow us here. Ain't no animal like that. It weren't real. Bettin' money they couldn't kill it. Can't kill that devil, ya know. Can't kill 'em."

"Keep your mouth shut if you don't have anything useful to say," John said. Turning to the woman, he nodded to the kitchen counter. "Got any more food? We've not eaten in a good while."

She started speaking, but she was so scared that all she could do was stutter.

John put one hand up and lowered the gun. "It's

okay, hun. What's your name?"

She glanced to her man before she answered. "Angel McGee. And my husband is Kevin."

"Don't worry. We're not out to hurt anyone. We just need a meal and a roof over our heads till dawn."

John and I could see their expressions change from fear to curiosity.

"Squatters?" I asked and Kevin nodded. With the Great Depression in full swing, folks who'd lost everything or never had much to begin with would find abandoned houses, ones that been foreclosed on by the banks, and just move in. It'd become a common thing, what with the number of homes sitting around empty.

Angel started rummaging through some boxes under the counter. In no time, she had the stove fired up. Mikey and I stared with watering mouths as she started cooking us some eggs and toast.

At first, I thought her cooking was just her way of being nice. Her side-glances at me and the others made it clear, though - the girl was terrified that we were gonna take advantage of her. Maybe her plan was to keep us busy with food instead of her lovely figure. Not that any of us were the 'taking advantage of' sort or in any shape to do anything like that, of course.

With our bellies full and us just glad to be resting

for a change, the night seemed to take on a peaceful aura. That being said and as it always does when you're on the lam, it passed as slow as molasses running down an icicle.

"What is that? It looks familiar," I heard Angel say behind me.

Looking back over my shoulder, I saw that John was holding up that damn ruby again, with Angel as entranced by the jewel as he appeared to be.

The light from the lantern flowed effortlessly through translucent stone, turning the far wall blood-red. Its cuts created a swirling, hypnotic pattern as it spun on the chain. The symbols, etched into the stone, could easily be seen on the walls. Thing was, they weren't red like the ruby, but seemed to have a slight yellowish glow.

John's eyes never left the ruby as he replied. "It'd better be something worth an ass-load of dough for all the trouble we've had today."

"He took it off some old lady in the bank," I said. "The old girl said her husband would make us burn for it. Pretty sure she was right."

John shot me an angry look.

"Mrs. Ruby," Angel whispered. She scooped out the last of the eggs on to my plate. "Not sure what her first name is, but her last name is Rubinstein. Everybody calls her Mrs. Ruby 'cause she wears that big old rock no matter where she goes."

Kevin shuddered. "Scary old bitch."

Angel giggled. "Daddy used to tell me that her husband, Harvey, was some big-time Indian-killer. He always said the old man was so good at killin' because he liked doing it so much. I think they said he died ten years ago or so. Story is that he got into a knife-fight with some moonshiners who were poachin' on his land and he killed most of them. She lives somewhere near Center Mountain. Comes into town every week or so for supplies."

My head jerked around to face my friend. "John, I think we oughta get that rock back to her."

He laughed, but I went on.

"I think she is right about her husband. We're being haunted, stalked by something that isn't human. That thing that got Jimmy, it wasn't right… I think it really did come from Hell. John, that thing was a demon of some sort. And Benny -"

"We're being hunted by the cops," John snapped. "Not haunted by a ghost. Stop actin' like a damn sissy. Jesus, my granny's got more of a dick than you do."

"Four-thousand three-hundred and ninety-three dollars," Mikey piped up. He smiled at his handy work. All the cash from the money-bag lay neatly stacked up on the floor in front of his crossed legs.

He rocked in place and looked up. "We lost, I'm guessing, another thousand in the car. I couldn't scoop it all up in time."

"Jimmy had a wife back home," I said. "I think she should get his share."

Mikey's words were fast and sharp. "No, I carried all of this. If anyone gets his share, it's gonna be me."

"We lost men, remember?"

I watched the shadows on Mikey's face contort as he looked up from the cash to meet my gaze.

Mikey's voice sounded almost diabolical as he spat out the words. "Then you two split Benny's share and I'll take Jimmy's share. Fuck his wife."

A loud crash tore through the room, and I jumped a foot off the ground as every window in the house slammed shut and exploded inward, showering the floor and all of us with glass. Hard winds whipped through the windows, as fast and furious as a tornado. Dust and dirt whipped up by the winds made it hard to see. All around me, the air looked alive, felt like a living thing trying to surround and smother me. I could see the dust collecting into smaller funnels, stretching around like snakes and spiraling to the center of the room, right where Mikey sat.

The whirlwind grew stronger as the currents of fast-moving air began to consolidate in the center of the room. I struggled to keep myself upright. John lost his balance and the wind sent him rolling several feet before he caught the door frame, keeping himself from being drug around the room and into the vortex. I finally couldn't stay upright and dropped to the floor, laying as flat as possible and keeping my hands over my head to shield my eyes from the sandblasting effects of the airborne dirt and debris.

Mikey's screaming made me glance up to look at him. The dust devil had swallowed him whole. Its vortex grew stronger around him, drawing in anything small and loose, making it appear almost like a solid creature. Dust and trash whipped around my friend, as well as all the cash that'd been on the floor.

I couldn't tell why he was screaming at first. I just thought it was him being terrified. But then the dust took on a reddish look and I suddenly remembered all the broken glass.

I could see the winds lifting him off the floor. Arms and legs would poke out of the little tornado, smeared and streaked with blood. All those sharp-edges were tearing into him, cutting him up like mad. I didn't know how much blood he'd lost, but it all swirled about him.

Angel screamed louder than any woman I've ever heard before and, just like that, everything stopped. The roaring noise disappeared, Mikey dropped to the floor with a thud, and the blood-soaked dust flew out in every direction. The air hung thick with it for a little while, a red vapor illuminated by the lantern which, surprisingly, still stood.

I cringed as red droplets fell and speckled my bare arms and face. I crawled over to where my buddy had fallen and regretted my move when I saw him up close. The sight forced me to turn and empty my stomach out on to the floor.

Mikey had been reduced to nothing more than a red pile of carved-up meat. His face was gone. Only dark empty sockets stared back at me.

"Move at all and I'll kill you!" Kevin hollered. His voice sounded unsteady but he held John's gun, which had been dropped in the mayhem and now was pointed at my last remaining friend.

John cautiously stood up and then turned, glaring at the man. He had a full six inches on Kevin and could take any of us in a fight, easily.

"Go on then, kill me," John growled, the ruby still clenched in his hand. He stepped forward with a smug grin on his face. "That thing's been jammed -"

He never finished the words. Kevin pulled the trigger and a dozen rounds shot out, making a straight line up John's gut to the top of his ribs. He was thrown back to the floor, his torso splayed opened and his organs burst out on display for all of us.

My friend, a man who'd been like a big brother,

just lay there. His open eyes looked up at me, as if pleading for a different reality, pleading for this nightmare to end. As they slowly closed, I feared I wouldn't live to see the sun rise.

Kevin turned the gun on me as I stood not knowing what to do or say. The weapon's barrel bounced due to the trembling hands that held it. His wide eyes held a look of panic in them. He'd taken a life and was mentally struggling to come to terms with that, as well as with the madness of the whole situation.

Kevin nodded over to John. "Hun, grab that rock outta his hand." He looked at me. "You just stay back there and don't move."

When Angel didn't move, he shouted the order again. It took a moment for her to grasp what was said, but Angel stepped over to John, her eyes careful not to look at the exposed organs. She pulled the ruby and chain from his dead hand and turned her teary blood-streaked face back to her husband.

In a meek voice, she announced, "Got it."

"Come on, baby." He sidestepped in the direction of the front door. He never let his gaze or the direction of the gun move away from me.

Bright lights and noise suddenly filled the room. Without warning, cars pulled up outside and their headlights bathed the little house in a white glow.

Dogs barked and the shouts of men echoed around the unworked farm. The posse must have found us and called for backup.

A man's voice yelled to us. "We know you're in the house. Y'all throw your guns out and just come out slow!"

Kevin pulled Angel over to him and looked back and forth between the door and me, not sure which was the bigger threat. The smile on his face told me that his mind was up to no good.

"Sit on the floor," he shouted to me. As I did what he asked, Kevin turned his attention to Angel. "Get that big knife off the kitchen counter and get behind him. If he moves, cut 'im. I'm gonna go outside and tell 'em that we caught 'em. Maybe there's a reward for them."

Reluctantly, Angel did as she was told and got behind me, the ruby still clutched in one hand and a knife in the other. At this point, I didn't care about getting caught, the nightmare just needed to end. The blood of two of my friends stained the floor, and I was having to sit in it.

Kevin started toward the door, then we heard the shouting again from outside.

"Don't make us come in! Step out here and make this easy on everybody!"

Kevin stopped and leaned the Tommy gun against

the wall, then pulled the door open, shouting back as he stepped into the doorway. "I ain't armed! I got a group of bad guys in here! They showed up a while ago!"

"Can't see your hands, get 'em up now!"

I was paying so much attention to him that I missed what happened until Angel's scream made me see it. Kevin turned around and his eyes widened in horror. Floating in the air a few feet away from him was the Tommy gun. It hovered, pointing at me as if someone held it at waist-level, but without warning, it flew at him. The gun hit him hard and flat across the chest. Out of reflex, he raised his hands to catch it. The force of the impact knocked him back into the open doorway, out onto the front stoop and visible to every cop out in the yard.

"He's got a gun!"

The police opened fire with everything they had - pistols, rifles, and their own Tommy guns. Their bullets tore into him. I couldn't make out the sounds of individual weapons, just one long continuous roar of thunder from the police. The impact of dozens of rounds pushed him back against the door, blood and bits of flesh flying out onto the front porch. Red spray burst out of his back in tiny short-lived jets. It moved through the air as if time had slowed it. He rolled to the side, staggering back into the room.

I don't know if his fingers tightened out of pain, or if some other sinister force was at work here, but the trigger clicked back and locked in position. The Tommy gun in Kevin's hands opened up in a spray of white fire. I threw myself flat onto the floor and looked up in time to see what happened to Angel.

Her body stayed upright, but jerked violently as each round struck her. One after another, every bullet fired tore into her body. Blood puffed out of her chest and back with each sickeningly thumping impact. Her blood rained down on me, coating my face and chest.

Yet she didn't move or fall as the gunfire continued to rain in on her. Then I noticed something horrific.

Smoke from the gunfire, as well as red mist pumped from her body, seemed to expose massive invisible hands, clutching her arms on both sides, as if a giant stood behind her, using her as his personal shield. Her eyes remained open, her jaw hung slack, and she appeared to feel nothing. Like a girl hypnotized by a stage magician, she seemed helpless and unaware of what was happening.

When the drum magazine on the Tommy gun ran its course, silence enveloped me. The ruby fell from her hand and hit the floor beside me. The thud it made on impact actually made me jump. I just looked at it, not sure what to do as she fell backwards onto the floor.

Kevin still stood in the doorway, still holding the gun. Still alive, he turned away from the woman he'd just killed and back toward the police. They began firing wildly into the house again. It looked like only a handful of the guns were aimed at him, with the rest determined to kill anyone or anything else in this shack. Plaster and splinters of wood flew everywhere, as did pieces of Kevin.

That damn ruby, I thought. I knew I couldn't leave it behind. As long as the haunted piece of shit was away from that old hag, people would die. I was the last one standing. I had to return it somehow.

Hearing a gargling noise, I looked up and saw Angel's eyes flickering as she coughed up blood. The poor thing was still alive. Maybe if I was gone and I took the ruby with me, the cops might get her to a hospital in time. So, I grabbed the damned thing and crawled as fast as I could to the backdoor.

I peeked out the partially-open door and didn't see anyone. It seemed they were all too focused on the front door. Taking a deep breath and praying for some luck, I ran out and hid in the tall brush, a dozen or so feet from the back stoop. My heart pounded and my lungs hurt from my heavy breathing, but I crouched down and wove my way deeper into the abandoned fields. I paused for a moment and looked back to make sure that I was safe.

A noise caught my attention and, a moment later, a couple of the cops came running around the back corner of the shack. Luckily, they didn't see me in the dark fields. Weapons at the ready, they started for the backdoor instead.

I gasped as the screen door opened and the bloody form of Angel walked out. The poor thing still had some measure of life in her and she had managed to get upright and stagger out.

My heart stopped. I couldn't imagine how she could still be on her feet after all of that. She looked like a lost and frightened little girl, mouthing unheard words, desperately trying to beg for understanding and mercy. To this day, I have no idea if she knew what was really happening in those final moments.

Already pumped up from Kevin's shooting, the men reacted immediately when they saw her coming through the back door. The two held double-barreled shotguns and they unloaded all their shells into her. Realizing what was going to happen, I turned away a split-second before the triggers were pulled. The poor girl had been caught up in our nightmare. She'd done nothing wrong except being in the wrong place. I couldn't watch that pretty thing literally being blown apart.

Dropping to the ground, I lay there and trembled

with fear, trying to digest what all had just happened. My friends were gone. A monster-like dog, floating guns, killer whirlwinds—It all seemed completely impossible, yet I'd witnessed them all.

My body shook even more violently as I replayed the images in my head. My body felt light and my stomach felt like it may purge whatever was left of Angel's cooking. Digging my fingers into the dirt, I shut everything out of my head and tried to relax. A deep breath, followed by another and another, finally started to ease the terror that gripped me.

Glancing around, only the brush-covered farmland, painted white and blue by the moon's light, surrounded me. I was by myself, completely alone in the dark with the Devil on the loose.

It took a couple of minutes before I remembered that I should be running. Hunched over, I walked quietly at first. I started running once I was far enough away that I wouldn't be heard. My feet didn't stop moving until the sun was up, and all I could think was the same thought, over and over again.

What am I going to do now?

FIVE

A narrow creek crossed my path, and the water did me a world of good. Kicking my shoes off, I waded into it, splashing the cool water onto my face. Stripping my shirt off, I washed myself, ridding my body of the layers of dried blood and dirt. Then I turned my attention to my clothes and washed them as clean as I could, but the blood stains had set and weren't coming out without bleach or lye.

Looking at the blood brought unwanted thoughts into my head. The shakes took over again. Dropping down into the water, I pulled my knees up close to my chest and I thought about the guys, my friends and comrades-in-arms.

That damn ruby felt so heavy in my pocket. I thought about pulling it out and throwing it as far away as I could, but I knew that wouldn't help. Angel said that the old woman lived near Center Mountain. I knew I had to go there. I had to return it. I was the only one left, and that meant I was next. From here on out, I'd be the target.

"Leave me be and I'll take it back to her!" I shouted and looked around for someone or something to direct my anger and fear towards. Tears began streaking my face and my words came out as pitiful wails of sorrow. "Can you hear me? Leave me be and I'll get it back to her!"

After walking for hours, another little farmhouse came into view. Caution didn't even occur to me as I approached. Figuring I could pass myself off as just another hobo, I checked the wood post that held up the mailbox. I only knew a few of the symbols that hobos used to identify places that were safe or unfriendly. It'd become common, with so many out of work, for men to walk from place to place, looking for a hot meal or work or a roof to sleep under, and the hobo code helped guide folks in these troubled times. This post was unmarked, so I had no idea what I'd be getting myself in to.

Crossing the yard and stepping up on the front stoop, I knocked on the door. My stomach roared with anticipation, but no one answered. I repeated the action and got the same results, so I strolled around the house, peeking in a couple of windows. Some clean laundry hung on a makeshift clothesline, spanning the distance between a pair of small apple trees. I snatched a pair of pants and a clean shirt and slipped them on. The pants hung a little loose, but my belt took care of that problem. The shirt fit perfectly and I rolled the long sleeves up to my elbows.

The two apple trees bore some worm-filled fruit. Quickly, I ate without caring about the bugs, they're nothing but protein, anyway. First one and then a second ended up in my stomach. I didn't want to overstay my welcome, so I figured I'd get back on the road. Before leaving, I grabbed another pair of apples, so I'd at least have something to munch on as I wandered on down the road.

An hour or so later, the sun's full fury had baked my exposed skin. It hadn't been this warm in a while and I wondered if this was some sort of punishment brought on by the ruby.

My hand slipped into the oversized pocket and caressed the jewel. Part of me toyed with the notion of pulling it out and looking it over under the bright sunlight, but a whisper from deep in my head told me not to. The idea that gazing into it had hypnotized John spooked me a little and I didn't want to take a chance of losing myself to its devilish power.

Rounding a bend in the road, I saw movement ahead. Two figures emerged from the brush that lined this portion of the road, a pair of boys who were out hunting. They were in their early teens and both wielded a single-barreled shotgun. One carried a beat-up leather satchel. A hint of rabbit fur poked out of the opening along the top.

I took a chance and spoke. "The hunting good today?"

One boy nodded to the bag. "Done killed three, so far."

"Rabbits?"

"Two of 'em, and I popped a squirrel too."

The other boy, who stood taller than the other, looked me over. I hoped he didn't recognize the clothes. He squinted his eyes. "Where you from?"

I tried not to stutter. I thought quickly and made up what I hoped would be a believable story. It just needed to sound convincing.

"Memphis. I had a ride on a truck for a while, but I got stranded out here. So now I'm on foot. I'm looking for someone local to these parts. She wrote my boss in Memphis, asking for work to be done on her house."

I hesitated and hoped they didn't ask too many questions. I wasn't sure I could keep up the lie.

The boy carrying the satchel, pulled it off his shoulder and sat it down as he spoke. "Least you didn't hitch a ride up with those bank robbers."

I cocked an eyebrow. "Robbers? Here? Didn't think there was a bank big enough 'round here to snatch anything from."

"The Sheriff drove by earlier letting us know they'd gotten 'em all last night, down the road a ways. They'd shacked up in an old house and the Sheriff's posse gunned them to Hell."

The other boy waved his shotgun around, making banging noises like a machine gun. "I heard the roar from those Tommys last night from my house. Must have been twenty of 'em, roaring and killing those folks, just like they do in the gangster movies."

I tried not to smile. "You don't say. Got 'em all?"

He nodded and I thought about it for a moment. I guess they didn't know that Kevin wasn't part of the gang, which meant that they weren't looking for me anymore. The cops would've known how many of us robbed the bank and how many were on foot - after all, we'd been seen running into the woods. Kevin and Angel were squatters, so the cops wouldn't have known they were living in the little house.

The weight of the world fell from my shoulders…

well, most of it anyway.

Clearing my throat, I decided to change the topic. I needed information on the old woman, namely where she lived. I thought for a moment on how to ask before I spoke. "There's an old woman that lives somewhere in these parts. My boss told me her name but I forgot to write it down. I remember he told me they called her Mrs. Ruby around these parts because she wears a big ruby around her neck when she's out and about. You boys wouldn't happen to know where she lives, would you?"

They gave me an odd look, obviously wondering why I wanted to see her.

Tapping the satchel with his foot, the taller boy spoke up. "Not sure which road she's living on, but Center Mountain is about ten or fifteen miles that way. I remember my dad telling me about her and her dead husband. They says he's a ghost and haunts that mountain."

The day wore on as I walked the lonely dirt road. The heat felt like it was drawing every drop of moisture out of me.

Sometime around mid-afternoon, I came across a

fork in the road. Luckily, a rickety signpost pointed me down the right path. In black letters on dirty white plank, someone had sloppily painted *Center Mountain - 5 Miles*.

I'd passed a few houses after leaving the boys, but the further I walked, the less the terrain showed signs of human encroachment. Even the road showed little signs of recent use. Eyes were watching me everywhere, but they didn't belong to humans. Birds, squirrels, and a couple of deer stared from the woods, either waiting to see if I were a threat or to see if I was prey for some unseen predator. I kept thinking they knew some unseen devil was stalking me, waiting to pounce when the time was right.

Hours passed in dreaded silence and solitude. The sun lowered in the sky, creating dark shadows in the woods and across the road. But the light streaming through the trees illuminated something new, something like mist or smoke. Stopping, I studied it and watched the light patches of vapor float by me. A smell of charred wood caught in my nostrils and my heart began to race.

I knew the smell of hickory burning. It'd always been one of my momma's favorite smells. As a youngster, she'd hand me some coins and have me walk several blocks to a market on the outskirts of Nashville to buy a bag or two of split logs. Pulling my wagon behind me, I'd do as she instructed and ask for only the best hickory. Old Man Perkins, who ran the place, would take the coins, help me load up, and then tousle my hair before I started the struggle of getting the wood home to Momma.

I didn't realize the memory affected me as strongly as it did until the tears had fallen as low as my jawline. Wiping them away and rubbing my eyes, I thought about Momma and my little sister, Lily. I'd walked out on them, left them to fend for themselves because I'd been selfish. Money, women, fame—I wanted it all and I ran away to get what I felt I deserved.

"I'll do good by you, Momma." I knew no one could hear me. Well, maybe the Lord could but with as thick as the trees were getting, I wondered if my words could even reach him. "I'll get the ruby back to the old bird and then I'll come home and make everything okay again."

With the sun dropping lower, I knew I'd need a place to sleep for the night. The extra apples I'd taken were already in my stomach and they'd not been enough to fill it up. Looking around as I walked, water and food were in short supply. No sign of a creek, no berries, no nuts, and I didn't have any way of killing a squirrel or deer, let alone of skinning and cooking them.

A second wave of smoke flowed through the trees and made my mouth water. It was hickory burning, but the scent was laced with something else. Maybe someone had a meal cooking. I thought about that, long and hard. The vapor trailed up a hillside and over the top. A thick layer of cold air, just above the tree tops, must have been keeping the smoke close to the ground.

Either it led up to sanctuary or it was an invitation to a trap. My hand slipped into my pocket and squeezed the ruby as I stepped off the dirt road and onto the wooded slope.

"I'm trying to return it. Just leave me be and let me get there," I whispered. I hoped that someone heard.

SIX

The angle of the slope didn't look bad at first, but with my body as worn out as it was, the muscles in my legs started burning about halfway up. Slowing my pace, I realized I'd hit the summit about the same time the sun dropped below the horizon. My eyes studied the hillside for a long moment, and I mentally plotted out the best route to take. Most, if not all, of the day's light would be lost shortly, and the last thing I needed was to be stumbling around up here in the dark.

The damn rock in my pocket seemed to weigh a thousand pounds as I wore myself out further, trying to rush up the remaining distance to the top. I wanted to curse and scream at the world, but I knew better. There wasn't any way of knowing who might be around.

As the ground began to level off, I found myself staring into nothing but darkness. The black air seemed unusually heavy and smothering.

I stood still and listened for sounds. In the distance, I could just make out a man's voice, but the words reaching my ears were nothing more than a mumble. The smoke smelled much stronger and I realized I must be close to the source. Training my eyes, I looked for some kind of sign - where there is smoke, there is fire, after all.

A yellow glimmer appeared in the far distance, across what looked like a shallow valley atop the opposite ridge. The light wasn't enough to illuminate my way or to illuminate anything else, for that matter. The flames produced just enough of a glow for me to see it from a distance, like a firefly that didn't blink on and off.

A controlled fire, hidden away this far into the woods could only mean one thing - moonshiners. The glow had to be a fire heating their still, or perhaps a campfire. A cold chill ran down my spine. Most shiners conducted their trade in secret, killing off anyone that might rat them out to the cops. Not that I wanted to see another damn cop again, of course, but I knew the shiners might not believe me. They honestly had no reason to accept the story of a stranger, especially a stranger that, most likely, wouldn't be missed this far away from polite society.

But my mind considered the other side of the coin. They had fire for warmth, water, and maybe food. And if I explained the bank robbery and running from the police, they may consider me a kindred spirit, just a man trying to make a living by breaking the law. My growling stomach helped that train of thought pull into the proverbial station.

Walking slowly, I moved toward the fire, trying my best not to make a lot of noise. The going was slow as I stumbled down the hillside and then back up the next. A foot at a time, the distance decreased and the light of the fire grew more exposed as I made my way to the top of the hill. Ahead of me sat not one but two stills, and big ones at that. Crates and jugs sat off to one side, while on the other was a rickety-looking cabin with a small campfire burning. Above the flames on a metal rod, I could just see what looked like a pair of squirrels roasting over the fire. The smell made my mouth water even harder and blinded my thoughts to everything other than eating.

I heard leaves rustling to my right. Spinning and snapping back to reality, I caught a glimpse of the butt of a gun, a half-second before it slammed into my face.

I didn't remember hitting the ground, but when

the stars stopped spinning, the twisted face of the attacker hovered over me, illuminated by the fire. The flickering yellow light made the man look demonic in nature. He hissed something I didn't understand through the dark gaps in his perverse smile.

Another voice yelled from the cabin, the voice of an elderly man. "Who is it? Anyone we know?"

A woman I could just barely see walking out of the cabin spoke up. "Is it Zeke? Did you just knock the sense out of your damn brother? He's supposed to be bringing me some peaches."

"This ain't him," the man standing over me answered.

As I stirred and tried to sit up, he shoved the twin barrels of his shotgun into my chest and pushed me back down. "Move again and I'll just blow a hole right through ya," he growled.

I stayed on the ground but lifted my head enough to see folks approaching. The woman came into view first. She dressed like a man. Only her long brown hair and ample feminine features made her recognizable as a member of the fairer sex. The lines on her face suggested she may have been in her mid-forties, but her slim athletic figure made her look far younger.

The man walking next to her must have been the one who spoke. Impossibly thin and sporting a shaggy beard and unkempt hair, he looked every bit as hillbilly as you could imagine.

In his wrinkled hand, the old man carried a sawed-off double-barreled shotgun, which was loosely pointed in my direction as he approached.

The old man waved the gun at the younger man. "Ducky, scout around and make sure he's alone. Go on. I got this jackrabbit covered."

My gazed darted to the younger man, Ducky. He looked around and I could see something bothered him. Fidgeting, he kept his gun trained on me.

Ducky's voice sounded high and his words came out quick. "Come on, let me plug him now. There's nobody else out there. If there were, they'd already be charging the place."

"Do what your Pa told ya," the woman said. When Ducky didn't act, she repeated it again, only louder and with some fire in her tone.

The young man relented and ran off into the darkness. I watched until he disappeared into the trees and then turned my attention back to the couple. They looked down at me with questioning expressions. Obviously, they were as confused to see me as I was to be in this whole situation.

"I'm not—looking for—trouble." My words sounded as shaken as I felt. I put my hands up. "I'm unarmed. Don't even have a knife."

"Get up," the old man said, acting annoyed rather than suspicious.

Standing, he motioned with the gun and I raised my hands again.

Both glanced at one another and then back to me.

"Check 'em out, Greta," the old man said to the woman.

Moving around behind me, Greta began patting me down. Her hands moved from pocket to pocket, coming to a stop as she felt the chunk of rock in the front of my pants, through the thin cloth. Her hand tried to slip into the pocket but my pants were a little too tight for her to reach the ruby at the bottom, thanks to the belt.

"Got no weapons, but there's something in his pocket." She smacked my ass. "Skinny little thing, ain't he?"

The old man lowered his weapon. "Where you from, boy?"

I jumped as Greta's hand squeezed my backside. "Nashville, originally."

The old man nodded and then motioned for me to follow him as he turned and walked to the fire. Greta smacked my ass again and spurred me on. Not being used to women being so forward, I stepped quickly away from her.

"Hungry, sweetie?" she asked, staying a few feet

behind me.

Looking back over my shoulder, I nodded. "Absolutely starving. Think I've only had a few apples over the past couple of days "

The old man grabbed an overturned bucket that sat near the fire and placed it a little closer before taking a seat on it. He pointed to another, indicating it was for me.

Following his lead, I took a seat. Suddenly, I felt the exhaustion that'd built up over the last two days crashing down on me. Dizziness caused me to sway slightly. Greta came up behind me, putting a hand on my shoulder and steadying me.

"Poor thing. Let's get some food in you." She began to move, but then the old man gave her a mean-looking stare.

The old man stretched his arms and rubbed his hands together, warming them. "So, you gonna tell me what you're doing out here, so late and far from home?"

Looking over at the man, I straightened up at the sight. The firelight created patches of almost pitch-black shadows on his face, contrasted by glowing pools of yellow. Greta remained behind me, her hand on my shoulder. The touch felt more like a restraint than a warm gesture. Feeling like I had no choice, I decided to just tell the whole truth.

"My friends and I hit a bank in -"

Greta interrupted me. "Hit?"

"Robbed. We robbed a bank in Memphis a couple of days ago and then another one in Millington." I watched the old man nod.

I continued, telling him about John's obsession with the ruby, taking it from the old bird, and then all the horrors that have followed.

"And now, I'm trying to get the ruby back to the old woman before that monster that haunts it kills me off."

"Mrs. Ruby?" Greta asked. "I think her real name is Rubenstein."

"I know her," the old man said, narrowing his eyes. His lips twitched into a smile. "So, all the others are dead? How much money you think you boys made off with?"

I shrugged. "Not sure. I know we had forty-two hundred when we'd reached the farmhouse, but that was all lost."

The old man's smile didn't fade, but I could see something in his eyes, something like a sense of loss. I knew he hoped that some part of the loot was stashed away in my pockets or boot. Easy money if he could get his hands on it.

The old man's smile widened and his eyes lit up. "Still got the rock, then? After all, you gotta have it if you're trying to return it."

"Was that what's in your pocket?" Greta asked in a playful tone.

Seeing the man's grip on his gun tighten, I saw there wasn't a choice. Slipping my hand into my pocket, I pulled the ruby out. Reluctantly, I held it out and held it over the man's outstretched hand.

"Ain't nobody out there," Ducky yelled out as he appeared from the tree-line.

Knowing they'd kill me, I decided to act. The old man had partially turned to look over his shoulder at Ducky. I jumped up at an angle, slamming into the old man and knocking him off the bucket and onto the ground. Greta tried to grab me, but I spun and got my hands on her arm. Jerking hard and extending my right leg, I tripped her up and sent her to the ground.

"Stop, boy!"

Glancing over as I broke into a run, I saw Ducky raising his shotgun. I charged for the woods with everything I had, taking care to shove the ruby back into my pocket. Two shots rang out in quick succession, shredding limbs and leaves just behind me.

Chancing another glance, I saw Ducky breaking the weapon open and trying to reload while stumbling forward in a partial run. I turned my attention back in front of me, just in time to see another gun-butt slamming into my chest.

The force of the impact stopped me in place, blasting all the air from my lungs. Stunned and in pain, my knees gave and I dropped to all fours. The man wielding the weapon stepped from behind a thick oak that'd given him cover and blocked my initial view of him. The gun-butt came down on the nape of my neck. The world lit up for a second or two and then everything in my messed-up world went black.

Seven

I couldn't be sure how long I was out. As consciousness returned, I found myself being dragged back to the cabin and the fire. Voices filled the night around me, arguing back and forth, but my mind couldn't focus on anything. The world seemed slow... at least, until I hit the ground face-first.

The old man rolled me over. Bent over, he grabbed my face, forcing me to look up into his eyes. "Now, boy, your mistake here was that you didn't think first. You acted before thinking things through and that's gonna cost you."

He laughed, and I slowly looked around at the people standing around me, staring down. A dark cloak of despair fell over me. They had numbers, guns, and they knew these woods. I had tired muscles, an empty stomach, and a chunk of crystal that was determined to kill me. Part of me wanted to give in, let them kill me so this whole nightmare would be done with.

The old man slapped the leg of the man who'd stepped out from behind the tree and hit me. "Good timing, Zeke. He up and surprised us. Didn't think he had it in him."

He shot the meanest side-eye at the other fellow.

"And you, Ducky, if you're gonna carry a gun around all the damn time, you need to figure out how to shoot it. Think those shotgun shells grow on trees? If I'm paying for them, you need to make your shots count."

Zeke must've been the brother that Greta had mentioned earlier. Peaches. She'd said something about him bringing her peaches. That'd mean he'd have been in town or at a nearby store. He might've known about the robbery and the gun battle at the farmhouse. At least, I hoped he'd heard something about it.

The old man said I acted without thinking. That wouldn't happen again. The seed of an idea appeared in my thoughts and, while the shiners argued about who did what, I ran a story through my head, over and over, working out details about how best to pull things off.

The old man held up the ruby and stared into the firelight that shone through it. "Boys, just take this piece of shit down into the valley and blast 'im. This rock will make us a fortune. I'm betting this thing is worth a year's shining-money."

"Chump change," I said, watching as every face turned to look at me.

Leaning towards me, the old man sneered. "What was that, boy?"

"Me and my boys buried one of our bags of cash in the woods after our car died. We hit two banks, we couldn't carry all of it. So, we buried most and carried enough to buy our way out of trouble, if we needed."

The old man scoffed. "How'd that work out for you?"

"You tell me. I know where there's ten-thousand in greenbacks, yours for the taking."

I slowly sat up. The folks all stepped back, three shotguns pointing down at me.

I feigned confidence in spite of the internal fearful screaming in my skull. "Question is, can we work out a deal?"

Greta glanced back and forth between me and the other men. "He's lying. He said they only had - "

I cut her off. "Yes, forty-two hundred in the one bag we carried with us. But like I said, there was a lot more. Too much for us to haul up and down these damn wooded hills."

"You're just full of shit," the old man said, getting ready to fire.

Zeke spoke up. "Maybe not. When I was at the general store, they were talking about the bank getting hit. They claimed the Sheriff bragged about getting the gang who'd hit the banks in Millington and Memphis. Said that the haul out of Millington was about seventy-five hundred. There could be something to his claim."

I stared down the old man. "Ten-thousand in greenbacks. I'll take you to it, and you let me walk away. Really now, do you think I'm going to go to the cops afterwards and say that a bunch of moonshiners threatened my life and took my stolen bank loot? You walk out of this with all the cash, and I walk away from here alive and well."

He looked around, obviously thinking about it.

I tried to add something to sweeten the deal. "You get all the money and the ruby, too."

The old man laughed. "You're damn right I'm keeping the ruby."

I winced a bit, but I tried not to let on. It wasn't just greed that had him fixated on the ruby. It was the dark power within that chunk of red crystal that had consumed him. Still, I'd have to tag along with them, pretending to show them the way back to the alleged burial site of the nonexistent money, and chances were that I'd watch the ruby destroy them as well, unless I could get away. They'd die if I couldn't. Last thing I needed was more blood on my hands because of that thing.

But all those concerns aside, this would give me a day or more's head-start in making an escape. They couldn't keep an eye on me every moment. After all, the stills couldn't run themselves - only a couple of them would be going with me, therefore less to worry about.

Looking up at the others, something odd caught my attention. I kept my mouth shut, but I watched as the tree limbs swayed in the wind. At first, only the tops of the trees moved. Then, in a deafening blast of air, the winds dropped to ground level, almost knocking everyone off their feet.

Greta's screams, barely audible over the roar of the winds as they began swirling about in abnormal ways, mirrored everyone's terror. While the men ducked down or dropped to the ground, she remained standing, rocking back and forth on her feet from the pressure of the currents. Leaves, sticks, dirt, and rocks all lifted from the ground and danced through the swift air currents. I saw the jagged inch-thick branch lift up, flying through the air currents, swaying from one current to another.

I screamed, "Greta! Duck!"

But I'm pretty sure that she couldn't hear me and, even if she had, I don't know if it would've mattered. Greta held her arms up and out. At first, I couldn't understand why, but as more dirt and leaves entered the volatile air currents, the real reason came into view. She wasn't doing it of her own accord. Instead, smaller currents, acting like tentacles or ropes, whipped around her wrists, pulling her into a position that rendered her helpless and vulnerable.

The branch danced in the wind, picking up incredible speed and finally speared her, tearing through her back and punching its way out of her chest. It emerged in a blur from her, along with copious amounts of blood and flesh, only to dart from one current to another until it was behind her again and repeated the process. The winds whipped faster, the branch moved faster, and Greta jerked violently each time she was hit, helpless and held in place by the winds.

She never screamed. After the first few seconds, I don't think she had the physical ability to do so. Within a minute, her chest had been riddled with so many puncture wounds that her torso broke apart. Her waist and legs dropped to the ground, spilling intestines and fluids everywhere. Her upper torso was lifted, high into the air, wrapped in dozens of air currents. They tugged and snaked around her eventually ripping her remains to shreds. Her head dropped to the ground, eyes and mouth open, staring at me as if frozen mid-scream.

"What the hell is going on?" Ducky hollered.

I looked over at him in time to see the currents grabbing him. He twisted and managed to get his feet on the ground. He struggled against the winds, but a massive collective burst of air hit him, sending him flying with the speed of a bullet into one of the stills.

Ducky hit the metal structure with such force that his body literally exploded a split second before the volatile liquid in the still ignited. The still blew apart in a massive ball of yellow flame. The blast proved strong enough that metal shrapnel ripped open its sister still, sitting next to it. The second still erupted into a fireball as well.

The old man, anguished and lost for words, reached for the stills.

Then he looked at me with Hell's fury in his eyes. "You brought this on me."

"The shine! The shine is on fire!" Zeke shouted.

I looked over at the crates just as one, then two of them burst open, spraying the ground around it with an invisible fire. Only the burning of leaves and the wood from the crates flamed up in yellow and orange.

Moonshine of a high quality burns hotter and

more intense than gasoline and, being invisible as well, this is one of many things that makes moonshining one of the more dangerous professions in those parts.

"No!" yelled the old man as he reached out to Zeke. The young man had jumped up and appeared to start running to the third and final crate. I figure he meant to pull it away from the fire, but he didn't make it.

He ran fast, ducking limbs and rocks, but the currents caught up to him. A blast of wind picked him up and threw the young man into the fireball that had once been the two stills. Seconds later, he emerged from the fire, his body covered from head to toe in brilliant yellow flames. I heard his screams over the roaring of the winds, but, luckily for him, they didn't last for long. He staggered out, making it halfway back to the old man before falling forward. He didn't move again.

The old man screamed obscenities at me as he stood and started to run. A few steps into his escape attempt, he threw the ruby at me. "Take it! You're the one it wants!"

A deafening roar made us both look around. The air currents moved, consolidated, and centered on the invisible flames from the broken crates of shine. In a flash of yellows and oranges, the leaves and sticks that were caught up in the wind monster burst into flames, burning up almost instantly. I lifted myself up, horrified. With all the debris burnt away, the dust became almost invisible in the night sky. Moreover, I saw massive spots on the ground flame up for an instant.

The old man looked at me and I realized at the same moment what it meant. The force had taken on a human-like form, comprised of invisible flame, and it was walking towards us.

Squeezing the ruby in my hand, I stood and ran for the woods. Something grabbed at my leg, tripping me up. Looking back, I saw a large branch fly out of the nowhere and slam into the old man's back, knocking him down. The fiery footfalls were close to him and I knew there was no chance that he'd get away.

I should've run, should've made my escape, but I couldn't. I was just too mesmerized by what was happening.

The dust within the creature took on a slight glow as the light from the fires at the stills poured through it. This allowed me to see the wind monster grab the old man and pull him to his feet. In a grotesque act, the monster basically hugged the man, pulling him inside of itself. Invisible flames ignited his clothing, providing plenty of light for me to see the old man being cooked alive. The roar of the wind all but left, leaving the man's calls as the only sounds, a torrent of agonizing shrieks that filled the woods and echoed down the valleys.

The flames were so intense that they roasted the old man within a couple of minutes. Only a horribly shriveled hunk of charcoal was left, falling to pieces as the monster released him. Stunned, it took a moment for me to see those fiery footfalls moving toward me.

Without hesitation, I jumped and started into the woods. Weaving back and forth, I did my best to stay ahead of it, but I had no light and I tripped several times, running smack-dab into trees. Looking over my shoulder, I could see flames on the branches, ignited by the monster as it chased me.

Pain shot through my legs from the constant twisting and falls. Finally, the slope became too steep and I fell forward, tumbling end over end, slamming my body into this tree then that one. The pain simply became too much for my body to deal with and I lost consciousness, falling into the blackness of the unknown.

EIGHT

A sweet song from an unknown bird awoke me. I immediately cursed the feathered little beast—my consciousness meant that I was aware of the pain reverberating from every part of my body.

Blinking from the intrusion of light into my formerly dark world, I found myself on my back at the bottom of a steep hill. Rolling my head back and forth, I thanked God for small favors. A foot to either side would have meant slamming my skull into the jagged rocks that seemed to be everywhere except where I was sprawled.

Looking up the hillside, I could see smoke, but no flames. My clothes and the ground around me were soaked. I laughed and gave thanks for the apparent overnight rain. Twisting and turning over, I mentally took stock of my physical state. Flexing my legs and arms, I gauged if there were any broken bones, but everything seemed fine and in working order, if sore as hell. With caution, I slowly rose and stood.

More birds began singing, dropping from the trees and rummaging through the wet leaves for bugs and worms. Looking up to the sky, I could see the sun just coming up over the horizon. At least I knew which direction was east and I still had a decent idea of the direction of the old bird's house.

Taking a moment to stretch, I replayed the events of the night before. Once again, everyone was dead except me. I realized that, if I couldn't make it, I couldn't go around anyone else ever again. The shiners may've planned on killing me, but that didn't mean that they deserved to die, especially in such horrible ways.

I walked for an hour before coming across a dirt road. The rain had turned it to mud, but it had dried in spots where the sunlight was able to reach through the leafy canopy. Looking at the weathered tracks, nothing appeared new. No one had traveled this road in a long while.

Another hour passed as I walked. The woods began retreating back, replaced by large swaths of farmland, some in use and some left to go wild. At least I knew I was back in civilization.

By noon, the August sun hung overhead and baked the dirt road and me along with it, but I kept walking. The humidity felt smothering, but I grew up in Tennessee, so this was nothing new

A small farmhouse rose up on the horizon.

Increasing my pace, I hoped to find some measure of help, food, water, or directions, but again, I thought about the shiners. Whatever help was available, it needed to be given quickly, otherwise people could die.

Getting close, a lovely young woman stood on the front porch, lazily sweeping. She looked up, saw me, and pulled the broom close to her chest. She also made a side-step closer to the front door.

"Excuse me," I shouted from the road. "I'm in need of some help. I'm looking for someone. Her name is Mrs. Rubenstein. Can you point me in the right direction?"

Nodding, the woman stepped to the edge of the porch and pointed. "Half a mile down the road, on the left. You'll see her private road. Walk that for a mile and you get to her house."

Giving a wave, I thanked the woman. Given her initial skittishness, I didn't press her for food or drink.

Walking quickly, the private road appeared right where it was supposed to be. Only a mile left to walk, then I'd be free of the ruby and, hopefully, the curse.

Eventually, the old manor house came into view. My heart pounded and I quickened my steps.

The air around me suddenly took on a bit of a chill. A light breeze played with my matted hair, tossing it around. I froze in place as dust began lifting from the road. It could be nothing, but still, I stopped and watched. My heart froze when I realized that the dust wasn't just blowing away. It began swirling around and around.

"No!" I shouted in despair. "I'm almost there!"

A dust devil came to life before my eyes, rising from the road and growing, but this one seemed thicker and stronger than the others I'd seen. More and more dirt lifted from the ground, consumed by the beast to give the windy apparition strength and bulk. It not only consumed dust and loose dirt, but small jagged stones all around seemed to defy gravity and shot through the air, disappearing into it.

It wasn't just a dust devil - the thing was a living creature and just kept growing larger, finally reaching twelve feet in height. Its winds grew stronger, concentrating on a single form instead of multiple tentacles. The dust devil roared like a locomotive. I couldn't hear a thing except for the cacophony of wind and the unnerving clacking sounds of thousands of rocks smacking into one another.

I started to back away and the thing moved

toward me. I swear I could see a face with black eyes forming and looking at me from inside the swirling mass. Then, like out of a nightmare, spiraling dust arms lifted from the sides and reached out toward me.

Without thinking, I pulled the ruby from my pocket and held it out. Some part of me hoped it'd just take it and go. The dust devil rushed forward and I could feel the strangest, painful sensation as one of the arms wrapped around me, the rocks within it tearing at my shirt and skin like a chainsaw. The pain tore through me. The scream I let out seemed to be sucked into the windy being. It was as if it fed on my scream, on my pain.

I don't remember how many times I left the ground, but I found myself being thrown repeatedly, bouncing back down onto the road, each time scratching my face and arms as I hit. Digging my palms into the road, I lifted myself only to have something impact my upper back, knocking the air from my lungs. Dust filled my eyes and I closed them, fearing that the flying trash would tear them from my skull.

Something in me broke at that moment, but not in a defeated way. No, some long buried part of me got angry. The lives of my friends, the shiners, and the couple from the farm house had been snuffed out without mercy or concern. All those people brutally killed because of a stupid ruby. Not one life was worth that damned thing, let alone ten. If I was going to die, it wouldn't be as a coward. Here was where I'd make my stand, my final stand.

Rising to my feet, I turned and balled my fists. "Enough! I didn't take the damn rock from your wife. I've done nothing but try and get it back to her. You've killed everyone around me for this!" I held up the ruby, letting it hang from its chain. "A stupid chunk of red rock!"

The dust devil roared and moved closer. Dropping to my knees, I grabbed a fair-sized rock and dropped the ruby to the ground. Holding the rock over it, I yelled, "I'll smash it if you don't get the hell out of my way! I said I'd return it, so let me do it!"

I didn't see him move at first. I only saw the blur of moment, a split-second before I felt his punch. It lifted me off the ground and sent me flying. The impact as I hit the ground left me momentarily dazed. Rolling to a stop, I lifted my head and looked at the ruby which lay several feet away.

I nodded to myself, feeling like I'd made the right call. I took a stand. I wasn't going to die as a coward.

Looking over, I saw the thing move closer, reaching out for me. I was too tired to run anymore. I had nothing to bargain with, no weapons, nothing but my dignity.

Pounding my chest, I rose to my knees.

"Come on, big guy. Do your best," I growled with all the hate I could muster in my tone.

"Let him go, Harvey!" a man's voice yelled over the roar.

The winds subsided, or so I thought. Wiping the dirt from my eyes, I realized that the dust devil had moved away from me. It hovered over the road, about twenty feet or so beyond the ruby, and watched me with those black eyes.

At least, I thought they were watching me. On a second look, I noticed they weren't focused on me but on someone behind me. Blinking hard to clear the dust from my vision, I turned and saw a cop standing a short way off. His wrinkled face had a look so fierce and intimidating that I wasn't surprised that the monster had moved away.

He glanced to me, then back to the monster. "It looks like the boy was returnin' what was taken. Now, get outta here and let me handle this from here on out."

I looked around at the dust devil. No... I looked around at Harvey, Mrs. Ruby's late husband. The swirling cloud stayed still as if it was considering its choices.

When it moved with an arm cocked back like a fighter prepared to swing a right hook, the cop did something unexpected. He drew his gun and pointed it at the ground near me.

Even over the wind, I could hear the hammer being pulled back on the huge pistol.

The cop didn't flinch. "I said... get out of here and let me deal with this."

I watched as Harvey slumped back somewhat. I could see that face again, this time with a wide toothy frown, the kind you might see carved into a jack-o-lantern. With a deafening roar, Harvey leapt forward, exploding outwards. Dust, rocks, and chucks of dirt rained out in all directions.

In muted terror, I fell to my knees and then slumped over on to the road, letting my tired torn-up body rest. I laid there for a bit and heard the footfalls of the policeman approaching.

He stooped beside me, laying a hand on my back. "You're gonna make it outta here alive, boy. Trust me on that one."

He helped me to my feet and I glanced around for the ruby. Finally, my eyes spied the spot where the cop's pistol had been aimed. He had meant to shoot and destroy it if Harvey didn't back down.

I couldn't help but laugh. "Never thought I'd say this, but thank God that a cop found me."

I hadn't mean to say it out loud.

He just chuckled, though.

He cocked a thumb at the road behind us. "Thank that cute little thing back that-a-ways. When you asked about Mrs. Rubenstein, she figured you'd run into trouble. She called into the station and they radioed me."

A short time later, I walked up to the old woman's front door. Grumbling somewhat, she stepped out to meet me.

"What do you want?" she asked me in the high squeaky voice.

I stood there, tired, covered in dirt and sweat, and scared to death. My trembling hand extended and opened to reveal the ruby. Her gaze went from it to my eyes and she squinted. A sly little smile formed on her wrinkled face. She leaned to the side and saw the cop sitting in his car. He'd been nice enough to drive me the last quarter-mile.

"Guessin' you ran into some bad times," she huffed. "Harvey always liked makin' a ruckus."

She took the ruby and watched as I turned to leave.

I had to know. "Was it really him?" I asked.

She nodded. "My husband liked fighting too

much when he was alive. No reason that death should be slowin' him up."

"What is it, the ruby, I mean?" My voice still shook, but not as much.

Squinting, she smiled. "Guess you can call it an anchor."

"I don't understand."

She leaned against the door and explained. "Harvey may have been a dirty fighter and a bad man, but he loved me with a fiery passion. I felt the same. For all his bluster, he feared losing me, in life and in death. I was the one thing he couldn't live without. So we pledged ourselves to always be together. We found us a spell-slinger to attach our spirits to the ruby."

That made sense, in a strange way.

I tried to fill in the blanks. "So when he died, his spirit stayed with the ruby and when you die, you'll be with him, attached to the ruby as well."

She nodded. "Good boy. As long as I have the ruby, we're together. And you seen what happens when someone takes it. Harvey finds a way to get it back to me."

A couple of nights of hell had taught me that lesson.

"What if the ruby is destroyed?" I watched her face sour at the words.

Her words came out as bitter as her expression. "Then his soul is set free to wander. No tell if we'd ever be able to find one another again."

"And the etching?" I asked but answered my own question. "Just part of the magic that makes this all happen, I suppose."

"Cost us a pretty penny, but it were worth it. We've been bound, soul to soul since Valentine's Day of '24." She sighed. "I'll be glad to get out of this life and see my Harvey."

She looked me over and appraised the broken man who stood before her. "Reckon you'll be rememberin' this the next time you think of stealin' what don't belong to ya."

I nodded and weakly answered, "Yes, Ma'am."

With that done, I walked back to the car and pulled myself in the passenger seat. Any and all desire to run had abandoned me. My body sank into the cushioned seat as the peace officer started the Ford and pulled away. I dozed off for a short while and dreamt of my friends and better times.

A hard bounce woke me up. Glancing around, I realized that we were not heading back into town.

"I've been the sheriff of this county for twenty odd years," the policeman said, eyes fixated on the road. "And by odd, I mean I've had to deal with Harvey several times before. By the time I got to the old Johnson house, you musta been long gone. Guess the boys didn't know about the squatters living there and assumed that fella was you, and that they'd gotten everyone in your gang. We knew how many were in your little gang of thieves from what the folks at the bank told us. When I realized we were a body short after all the mess and the ruby was still gone, I figured I knew where to look for you, assuming you were the smart one of the bunch.

"Old Mrs. Ruby back there, she wears that damn rock all the time. You aren't the first to have taken it and everyone who has... well, old Harvey makes sure they don't get too far away."

He pulled the car off to the side of the road and looked at me. "You got any cash?"

I shook my head. He reached into his pocket and pulled out a couple of notes. Handing me the money, he said, "This is the county limits. There's a little town 'bout half a mile up the road. You should make it before the sun goes down. They got a bus that makes a run from Texas to Nashville. It usually pulls in about seven or so."

"I don't understand," I stammered. "Aren't I going to jail? I robbed a bank."

He lit a cigarette and squinted at me through the smoke. "Boy, you got four dead friends and you've seen some seriously messed up shit over the past forty-eight hours. Do you think a little jail time is going to do you any more good? Hasn't this trip through my town scared you straight?"

"You have no idea how straight it's scared me."

"Go on. Start a new life. Make something worthwhile out of yourself."

I stepped out of the car and looked back through the window at the cop. He gave me a nod and that was that. I caught a bus and never looked back.

NINE

Jerry's Bar, 1951

I swallowed the remainder of my drink and looked at Natalie. Those beautiful eyes looked right through me, showing no expression as she considered my story. I guessed that deep inside she was telling herself that I'd made up the whole thing.

But a hint of fear showed through my words, just enough that she just didn't want to believe it, more than anything else… didn't want to believe that Harvey was real.

When she spoke, she sounded surprisingly sad. "In a strange way, it's a love story. Bound together on Valentine's Day."

"That's one way of looking at it."

"It's pretty late," she murmured. "I guess I should go. Thank you for the drink and the story."

Natalie scooted to the edge of the seat as if she wanted to go. Standing, she took a single step toward the door, but then she glanced back. I could see it in her expression. She hoped I'd want her for the evening, hoped to have someone who'd treat her nice. Maybe she was just lonely. Even a hooker needs someone who'll hold her and expect nothing more than to just lay still and enjoy someone else's company. Everyone needs a shoulder to lay their head on, once in a while.

Sex would be nice, but I preferred the thought of feeling the warmth of a woman in my bed again. Nothing erotic, just someone to hold. Reaching out, I took her hand and pulled myself up. Running a hand in my pocket, I withdrew a couple of bills and tossed them on the table to cover my tab.

Pulling out a business card and a pen, I jotted down a number on the back. Natalie slipped on her jacket and, in the process, I watched those curves being hidden away.

"I'm a couple of blocks away," I said as we stepped out into the cold night air. "It's not much, a single bed at the West End Building."

After handing her the card, I slipped on my jacket and hat. A hard breeze hit, requiring a readjustment of the aged fedora.

"I don't understand," Natalie said, reading the figure on the back.

"That's your salary, if you take the job."

She narrowed her eyes. "And what are you hiring me for? Or should I ask, how long are you hiring me for?"

I thought about it for a long moment. The few friends who knew me well had expressed concerns over the last few months about the path I'd staggered down. I heard all their worries and complaints as I composed my thoughts.

Exhaling, I stopped and looked her in the eyes.

"At the end of my story, after making things right with Harvey, I found that I needed to leave my old life behind, make a fresh start and take a different road to something better. Since my wife died, I've been walking in the wrong direction, drinking too much and not giving my job one-hundred percent. I need to fix things, so getting my professional life in order would be a start. And to do that, I need a secretary."

I motioned to the card. "You'll get that amount every week. I have an office nearby and you'd do the normal kind of office things."

"I don't know a thing about being a secretary."

"I've never had one, so I don't know what to

expect either. Some typing, I suppose. Answering phones. Keeping me in line. I mean, anything you do would be a help. The bar is pretty low, so I'm sure you'll do fine. Assuming you want it."

She stared at the card with a goofy grin on her face, then she looked up at me. "So you made a fresh start, then."

"Yep."

She took my hand as we walked and squeezed it tight. She cleared her throat and asked, reluctantly, "Did you ever steal again? After that night, I mean?"

I rubbed my eyes and thought of my lost friends.

"Never done a wicked thing since. Well, not intentionally, that is. Well, maybe I have, but I only do bad things to bad guys. Vampires, werewolves, witches, and all other forms of evil lurk in the shadows around here. Maybe if I help enough people deal with the creatures of the night, the guilt of wasting those years, losing my friends, and being a stupid little snot will go away and let me sleep a little better at night. And I've not even told you about the war. Talk about a nightmare."

"Guilt? It wasn't your…" She started but stopped, then took a different direction. "War? Japs or Germans?"

"The Japs, but they weren't the only monsters in the Pacific."

She cocked an eyebrow. "Oh really?"

I nodded.

She took a slight side-step, nuzzling herself against me as we walked. "I think I'm starting a new path?"

"You plan on continuing to walk these streets?"

She playfully punched me in the arm. "No, silly. But if it's okay, I may keep dancing. The extra money wouldn't hurt, and I enjoy it."

She looked concerned. "I hope that isn't a problem because I don't plan on stopping. At least until I get a singing gig somewhere."

"Dancing at the club? Nah, that's fine with me, as long as you enjoy it. Just do me a favor and stay away from Voodoo Rumors."

"Oh? I heard about the place. They say the woman who runs it is a witch. Some say she's a real demon or something. You know her?"

I snorted. "You could say that. She's my sister."

"Your sister is a demon?"

I couldn't help but laugh. "It's a long story."

We didn't talk for a while. We just listened to the street performers as we walked. They were on every corner, filling the city with song.

"Think Harvey is in hell now?" she asked, quietly.

I couldn't help but chuckle. "No. I'm sure he is watching over that old bird, no matter where she is.

But as mean as that old boy is, I'm betting that even Satan couldn't keep him locked up all the time, if he were there. But I don't worry about seeing him again. The afterlife doesn't scare me anymore. That night and many others like it since… I've done my stint in Hell."

I shot a quick glance at my watch. Both hands clicked together, facing upwards and the date in the tiny window finished its turn and read fourteen.

"Happy Valentine's Day." I said.

She turned and smiled. "You know what they say about meeting someone new on Valentine's don't you?"

I shook my head, smiling at the giddy expression she wore.

"Those relationships last forever, ruby or not."

About the Author

Chattanooga native, D. Alan Lewis's debut novel, *The Blood in Snowflake Garden* was a finalist for the 2010 Claymore Award. Alan's other novels include, *The Lightning Bolts of Zeus, Keely,* and *The Bishop of Port Victoria*. He is the editor of four anthologies from Dark Oak Press, *Capes & Clockwork 1 & 2* and the 2 *Luna's Children* volumes. Alan has numerous short stories published, and won multiple awards for his steampunk short stories and novellas. He is a frequent speaker/guest at various genre conventions and runs writing & publishing workshops.

You can follow Alan at his website: **www.dalanlewis.com** Or on Facebook: **Author-D-Alan-Lewis** Or on Twitter: @Dalanlewis

Bonus Chapter:
The Last Encore — Voodoo Rumors 1951
Book 2
Chapter One

West End Apartments, Nashville
Tuesday, February 1951, 5:59AM

A well-worn album spins on the rickety old turntable, giving off a steady rambling of pops and scratches that matches my breathing. God only knows how long ago the last song ended. I've been listening to the jazz without really hearing it, but just knowing it was there, just outside of my focus, brought some sense of comfort to this worn-out soul.

Something about it... the steady tempo, the simple-yet-powerful lyrics, or even the wicked guitar riffs, perhaps, seem to tell my story. All of his songs tell my story. Every song on the album has a strong sound with a great blend of guitar, piano, and just the right amount of percussion, and all that was topped off by a voice that's seen me through too many troubled times.

This night has been one of those troubled times,

and I worry its aftermath will stay with me for longer than usual. That is, if it ever leaves me at all.

From my vantage point, I can see the slight pinkish glow in the eastern sky bringing a measure of warmth to the early frost that's fallen on Nashville. A pair of long thin clouds that look like brilliantly lit coils of yarn hang over the horizon, barely visible over the buildings of the Vanderbilt campus.

My mind is drifting to and fro, not wanting to linger on anything for too long. Too much has happened tonight for me think of only one thing, but it was one man in particular that really mattered.

It's been a bad night, the only solace to be found in a now-empty bottle that sits beside me on the fire escape outside my bedroom window. The cool February winds stings my face, chilling the wet streaks running down my cheeks. My sweat-soaked T-shirt feels almost frozen, but a belly-full of Jameson keeps my insides burning like torches wielded by a thousand angry villagers.

I hear the clicking of a key in the door's lock, but I don't bother looking. I know it's her. Natalie knows about the case and what I had to do to wrap things up. It'd become customary for her to come by my apartment each morning, after nights when I've worked. 'To check up on me' or 'patch me back together' are the usual reasons she gives.

Natalie usually sleeps in late, coming into the office around ten or eleven, but on nights I've worked, she makes it a point to get up early. Personally, I don't think she's slept at all on some of these evenings. Nothing about our twisted, complicated relationship is fair to her.

After meeting her one night at Jerry's bar, I offered her a job as my secretary. In retrospect, it seemed silly to give someone a job, considering I rarely use my office or even step foot in it for weeks at a time. I've always had it as a meeting place for clients but, since most jobs come through the Nashville Police Department, I rarely make use of it. When I saw her that first time, though, I decided things needed to change. My career needed a boost, my alcohol intake needed to lessen, and a hooker needed a real job. So, she came to work for me and, on occasions, danced at one of the local clubs for extra money.

She didn't take the secretarial job because she wanted to make an honest living… she wanted me, body and soul. I just couldn't give it to her. Not yet anyway. The people I'm closest to tend to end up paying a heavy price for loving me and I couldn't handle that kind of cost being levied against her young soul, not for the sake of the attentions of a middle-aged man like me.

I sit still as she approaches, leaning out the window, looking me over. Her eyes move from the empty bottle to the bloodied makeshift bandage around my left arm to the smoldering cigarette I hold loosely between my fingers. Somewhere inside it, strands of tobacco still burn, but an inch of ash hides their glow.

A hand, so soft and delicate, reaches through the opening and touches my face, sliding along the salty chill. Her fingers move up my arm and hover over my shoulder, where a bullet wound has started seeping blood again. A matching wound lays just out of her view on my left thigh.

No words are spoken as she climbs out, scooting on her backside until she's pressed up against me. Her arm snakes around my tired body, pulling me over so that my head rests on her shoulder. We sit together and watch as the world lights up.

Some nights, I vanquish evil from my city, but I never gloat over that fact. Whether it's putting down a werewolf, staking a vampire, or killing whatever form of evil stalks the streets, it's my job. The church told me that I'm doing God's work... to some degree, anyway. Now and then, a surge of satisfaction takes hold of me when I see a monster dead at my feet, but most times, the killings take something out of me, like a little piece of my soul has been torn away and spirited down into the depths of Hell for demons and devils alike to feast upon.

Tonight, it's one of the most-times, and it feels like far more than a little piece has been taken.

The world of Thomas Dietrich is about to get bigger. Keep reading and explore the dark, seedy side of America's Music City.

Voodoo Rumors – 1951

The Blood Red Ruby – available now
The Last Encore – coming March, 2017
A Penny for Luck – coming Summer, 2017
Wild Pooch – coming Fall, 2017
Doomsday, The Devil, and a girl named Betty – coming Fall, 2017
Dietrich's Inferno – Coming Winter, 2017

GUNFIGHTS, AIRSHIPS AND BULLET-PROOF CORSETS ARE JUST PART OF THE JOB FOR AMERICA'S PREMIERE STEAMPUNK SPIES.
Hawke Girls
THE LIGHTNING BOLTS OF ZEUS
BOOK 1 OF THE HAWKE GIRLS' ADVENTURES
BY D. ALAN LEWIS
AVAILABLE ON AMAZON.COM OR YOUR LOCAL BOOK SELLER.

Made in the USA
San Bernardino, CA
02 March 2018